CHASING HER TRUST

DARE TO SURRENDER
BOOK ONE

DANIELLE PAYS

Chasing Her Trust
Copyright © 2020 by Danielle Pays

All rights reserved.
No part of this book may be reproduced in any form or by any electronic or mechanical means including information storage and retrieval systems, without written permission from the author, except for the use of brief quotations in a book review.

This is a work of fiction. Names, characters, places, and incidents are the products of the author's imagination or are used fictitiously. Any resemblance to actual persons, living or dead, business establishments, events, or locales is entirely coincidental.

All rights reserved.

Edited by: R. C. Craig
Cover by: Maria @ Steamy Designs

www.daniellepays.com

Chapter One

A pungent spicy scent overwhelmed Nick Moore as he entered the small grocery store. Glancing down, he noticed pumpkin candles were on sale next to the door, so he hurried to the back to escape the smell and looked around for bread. He would have preferred a frozen pizza, but his motel room didn't exactly come with a kitchenette.

"I said no. Can't you just listen for once!"

He heard the woman's voice coming from the aisle beside him. As she drew closer, he quickly became deeply interested in the cans of pure pumpkin stacked in front of him. More pumpkin. What was it about fall that made everyone go crazy over pumpkins?

"Figure it out yourself. I'm done."

Her insistent tone reminded him of his ex.

She'd also been overly demanding with expectations he could never live up to.

"Ugh!" the woman yelled out as she rounded the corner, tossing her phone into her purse.

Suddenly, red lights flashed, and a maniacal laugh rang out from an animated skeleton on a Halloween display, and she jumped, dropping the basket she was holding.

"Godammit!" She kicked the skeleton, causing it to tumble to the ground, which set off another round of the creepy laughter from the floor. She kicked it again.

Nick couldn't help but chuckle as he watched her throw the temper tantrum. That caught her attention, and when her head snapped up, her amber eyes met his. She had on almost no make-up and he could see a faint scattering of freckles on her face. Her blond hair fell just past her shoulders and despite the fact that she was wearing a baggy sweatshirt and jeans, she was sexy as hell.

"Something funny?" she asked.

He grabbed her basket off the floor while he got his laughter under control. "Not at all." His gaze roamed over her body, and when his eyes made their way to hers, she was glaring at him.

Damn. She'd caught him checking her out.

She jerked the basket away from him, and when her fingers grazed his, it sent a tingle up his arm. He grinned, not able to remember the last time he'd had a physical reaction like that right after meeting a woman.

"Nick Moore." He held out his hand.

"No, thank you," she said as she sidestepped past him.

"I was just introducing myself."

She spun around. "Your eyes were doing more than that." Then she turned away from him to leave.

He couldn't help but grin. Well, damn.

"You're welcome!" he shouted after her.

Without missing a beat, the woman held her hand up behind her back and slowly extended her middle finger.

Yep, he knew her type. His ex had been the same and he'd experienced enough princesses in his lifetime. It didn't matter how great it had felt to touch her—that probably had more to do with his lack of a dating life this last year.

"Did you say you're Nick Moore?"

Nick swiveled around to find a tall, lanky man in a police uniform standing behind him.

"Yes."

The man stared at him. "You're the detective taking over Joey's position." It wasn't a question.

"Who's Joey?" Nick studied his uniform closely. The badge read "Harvey, Fisher Springs Police Department."

Harvey quirked a brow. "Chief's boy. He's on a medical leave of absence. It's temporary, so don't get too comfortable here."

Temporary? When he interviewed for the position, the chief never said anything about it being temporary. Not that it mattered. He only planned to stay in this small town for six months. He was certain that after that, he'd be able to get his previous job back with the county sheriff. By then, his old boss would be begging for him to return. He was one of their best detectives. If not for that incident on the Morgan case, he'd still be there.

"Thanks for the welcome, Officer Harvey."

"Didn't say you were welcome." Harvey crossed his arms.

The guy was acting like Nick had taken Joey's job. Maybe if he played along with the temporary aspect, Harvey would warm up.

"Good to know. When's Joey coming back?"

Harvey narrowed his eyes. "Not sure."

Nick rocked back on his feet, then caught himself. It was a nervous habit he'd picked up when he was in the service. One he thought his drill sergeant had worked out of him. But here he was, rocking like a nervous fool.

Enough of this. "Looks like we'll be working together, Harvey." Nick held out his hand.

The man ignored it and shook his head. "We'll be coworkers, but I doubt we'll work together."

Nick opened his mouth to respond, but the man pushed past him, bumping his shoulder as he went.

Nick suppressed his laugh. A move like that might have been intimidating coming from a large man, but he had a good couple of inches on Harvey. Hell, at six foot three, he had a few inches on almost everyone.

He needed to find out who Joey was and if he was coming back. While stewing in his thoughts, he finished his shopping and paid for his food without meeting any other locals.

Stepping outside, he took a deep breath of fresh air. Sweet relief from the pumpkin infused building. He could only imagine how overboard they'd go for Christmas. There was a crisp fall chill that said snow could come at any time, yet the sun overhead warmed him.

After loading everything in his trunk, he caught sight of the blond, now pushing a cart with a case of water bottles across the parking lot. He knew he shouldn't stare, but he couldn't help it. Despite her rudeness, he found himself drawn to her. For a moment, he wondered if she'd seen him, but when she walked her cart down the opposite side of the aisle, only to take a sharp right to get to her vehicle that was merely two away from his, he was sure she was avoiding him on purpose.

He should get in his car and leave. But he didn't. He watched her. Then she reached down and tried to pull the case of water from the bottom of her cart. It didn't move.

"Damn it," he said under his breath. Now he had to go to her. He couldn't stand seeing her struggle, so he rushed over.

"Let me help you with that." He grabbed the water from her hands and yanked. It was hung up on the front of the cart. He yanked again and when it came loose, he moved it into the trunk.

"What are you doing?" Her arms were crossed, and she was glaring at him.

"I'm trying to help you out." Crossing his own arms, Nick matched her stance.

Her eyebrow quirked. "I didn't ask for your help."

"But clearly, you needed it."

Her arms immediately went to her sides, her fists balled up. "It wasn't heavy. It was caught on the cart. I would have gotten it just fine."

He shook his head. "Damn, you ball-bust all men?"

"What the hell are you talking about?" Smoke was practically coming out of her ears. She slammed her trunk shut.

"I heard you in the store. Sounds like your boyfriend tolerates a lot more than I would." What the fuck was he saying?

"*Than you would*? You're a piece of work." She moved toward the front of her car.

"Me? I'm merely trying to be a gentleman—"

She was in his face before he could finish. "No, a gentleman would have asked if I needed help. You swooped in, took over, and then insulted me."

He'd wasted enough time already, so he refrained from saying anything else. He had a motel room to get back to and a peanut butter and jelly sandwich to eat.

"If you see me again, please walk the other way." With that, she got into her car and drove off, but before she pulled out of the parking lot, he noticed a colorful stuffed animal in her back window, which didn't fit at all with her ball busting personality.

Welcome to Fisher Springs, he thought to himself. He was zero for two on his first day here. Hopefully, the rest of the town would be more welcoming to their new detective.

Chapter Two

Lauren Harrow drove her Honda Accord out of the lot of Tim's Grocery and stewed for the entire five-minute trip to work. She'd give anything to not have to deal with another man. Ever. First her ex, Scott, wouldn't leave her alone. Then that guy at the store. Nick Moore.

The way he spoke sounded so formal. There was no way he was from Fisher Springs. No one was formal here. She let out a sigh of relief. At least that meant she probably wouldn't have to see him again.

When they first locked eyes, she believed she felt something, but then he turned out to be a pushy asshole, like Scott. And with that, her thoughts returned to her ex's phone call. Why was he so intent on winning her back? He certainly hadn't wanted her when they were together.

Whatever the reason, it didn't matter. She wasn't going to take him back. Instead, she tried to focus on the spooky decorations that adorned all the shops on Main Street. With Halloween so close, it meant it would soon be the holiday season. Her best friend, Harmony, had explained how the entire downtown area transformed into a magical place for the kids on Halloween. Since this was her first time in Fisher Springs during the holidays, she planned to check it out and enjoy it.

When she pulled into the parking lot, her mind drifted to the grocery store again. But this time, it wasn't Scott she was thinking of when she slammed her car door closed and marched toward the diner. No, it was Nick. Arrogant, pushy, yet sexy as hell Nick. She tried to put him out of her head — the only reason he was still there was because she hadn't been with a man in months. And whose fault was that? Scott's. She'd finally stopped trying because he'd turned her down so many times.

Harmony arched a brow at her as she stomped through the door of the diner.

"Scott." That was all Lauren needed to say.

Then she headed toward the back room, Harmony following close behind, where she tossed her coat into her locker and pulled off her sweatshirt, trying not to catch a glimpse of herself in the mirror. The pink T-shirt she had to wear for her uniform was a bit *too* pink for her taste, but at least it was easily hidden under her other clothes.

Harmony leaned against the lockers and crossed her arms. "What happened?"

"He called me again. Why won't he leave me alone?" she said as she tied an apron around her waist.

Harmony put her hand on Lauren's arm. "You told me he cheated on you, but you never gave any details. Could it have been a one-time thing that he seriously regrets?"

Lauren squeezed her eyes shut. The image of Scott with his pants around his ankles and his assistant bent over his desk flashed in her mind. Nausea came boiling up. She hadn't wanted to say it out loud, but maybe if she told Harmony, she could work past it. Harmony was her best friend in this town. Thank God she'd met her when she moved here last month. This place could be awfully lonely to outsiders.

"I literally caught him having sex with his assistant. And trust me, it wasn't a one-time thing."

"Oh shit, Lauren. I'm so sorry."

"Then today on the phone, he had the nerve to say I misunderstood! Can you believe that?"

The sudden desperate expression on her best friend's face raised her suspicions.

"Okay, spill it—what's wrong?" Lauren asked, almost afraid to hear the answer.

"About Scott..." Harmony bit her lip and

stared at her.

Impatience won out. "What about him?!"

"I heard he's in town again. For good."

Lauren fell into the chair next to the lockers. Her heart was racing. "No. He said he'd never return. He can't. I have nowhere else to go."

"Well, brace yourself because Ms. Finkle came in earlier and said she heard he's back."

This was the last thing she needed. Scott Fisher was loved around here. And it didn't help that the town was named after some relative of his. Or that he'd been the captain of the football team and could do no wrong in the eyes of everyone who lived here. Lauren had met him during one of her visits to Fisher Springs on summer break in college and they'd hit it off.

That is, until her mom died a few months ago. She'd needed comfort, but it seemed that Scott had always needed to work extra hours. Now she knew what he'd really been up to. The image of Scott with that woman flashed in her mind again.

"He's not the only guy making news in town. I heard the new detective showed up at the grocery store and caused quite a stir. Peggy said he is one delicious man. She said his name is Nick." Harmony headed toward the dining room.

The bell over the door jingled, and Lauren passed her friend as she walked out to the front. Looking over her shoulder, she asked, "Nick Moore?"

Harmony's eyes widened. "Yes! Have you seen him? Is it true? God, we need more men in this town."

"Don't get your hopes up. Nick Moore is a sexist jerk."

"I agree—he's a jerk all right."

Lauren turned at the sound of the new voice and found Harvey standing at the front counter with his hands on his hips. "Besides, you want a good man? I'm right here." He grinned at Harmony.

She swatted his arm. "I'm not talking about my best friend. I'm talking about a man I can have hot monkey sex with."

Harvey's face flushed as he shifted on his feet.

Interesting, Lauren thought.

"Lauren, you say this Nick is a jerk?" Harmony asked.

"That's right," Harvey answered for her.

"Sounds like the perfect rebound guy to me. He probably won't stick around this town, so you can keep it short and sweet."

"The last thing I need in my life is another guy," Lauren told her and then said to Harvey, "Nick already managed to offend you too?"

Harvey nodded. "Anyone who takes Joey's place offends me. I'm happy to see you aren't blinded by his charms. Maybe there's hope for us after all." He reached over and tucked a piece of hair behind Lauren's ear while glancing at Harmony. Lauren backed away from him.

Harvey had been flirting with her ever since Harmony introduced them, and this made her wonder whose benefit the flirting was actually for. Glancing at her friend, she noticed she was wearing a scowl just before plastering a smile on her face as she stepped past Lauren.

"Hey, Harvey. Any crazy stories today?" Harmony asked.

"No. Ms. Finkle must have kept her cat inside."

They both laughed.

From the time she'd met Harmony and Harvey last month, Lauren had been amazed they weren't more than friends. They were always laughing at each other's jokes and seemed to have a real connection. But when Lauren asked Harmony about it, she explained that she'd known Harvey since grade school. There was no mystery.

"Well, no stories, no dinner," Harmony told him.

"You're something else, Harmony. All right. How about an oldie but a goodie?"

Harmony clapped her hands together and sat down. "Yes! I love the classics."

"You want to hear this too?" Harvey was looking up at Lauren.

A woman walked into the diner rubbing her arms. "Oh yes, heat. It's so cold out there!"

Lauren glanced back to Harvey. "Go ahead

and tell your story to Harmony. I'm going to help this customer."

No offense to Harvey, but Lauren could use all the work and tips she could get. She wasn't sure how much longer she could stand to stay in the Chanler mansion.

★ ★ ★

Several hours later, Lauren collapsed onto the chair in the back room for her break. Images of Nick's arms flexing as he forced that water out of her shopping cart filled her mind. She'd tried not to stare, but his shirt had done little to hide his muscles. And those jeans had looked like they were painted on. She shook her head. No, she wasn't this hard up. Although it'd been months since she'd had sex — which should have been her first clue something was going on with Scott. He never used to turn her down. But toward the end, he always claimed he was too tired. Now she knew the truth.

The bell over the front entrance rang. She checked her watch. Not too many customers came in this late on a Monday night.

Then she heard the familiar voice. Jumping up, she ran to the door and peeked down the hallway to the main dining area.

Scott was here. Shit, shit, shit. She started

pacing. She wasn't ready to see him yet.

Harmony snuck into the room. "Go out the back. I'll cover for you and tell the boss you got sick."

"Are you sure?"

Harmony pushed her friend toward the lockers. "Yes, but hurry. Scott saw your car in the lot. That's why he came in. I can only distract him for so long."

Lauren threw her arms around her friend. "Thank you!" She grabbed her purse and ran out of the diner.

For the entire drive home, she wondered why Scott wanted her back. Things hadn't been good for a while and he hadn't shown any interest in fixing anything then. Why now? Why hadn't he come after her last month when she left?

The white pillars that lined the porch came into view. The house was ridiculous and stood out in a town like Fisher Springs. But regardless, the sight of it brought another wave of grief. This was the last place her mother had lived, the last place she'd called home before she died, and going down the long driveway always made Lauren think of her. Tears fell as she reminded herself that it was only temporary. And as much as she didn't like it, staying here did help her feel closer to her mom.

After parking her car out front, she steeled herself for the run to the door. Everything about this sprawling property creeped her out. It wasn't only located outside the small town, but it was also surrounded by trees, and there was little outdoor light. Michael, her stepdad—if she had to call him that—had insisted on no outdoor lights because it interfered with his ability to stargaze. Staring up to the sky, she laughed. The regular cloud cover here made stargazing nearly impossible.

Okay, she could do this. She quickly ran up the porch steps, ignoring the howling that she could only imagine was a pack of wild coyotes ready to pounce. As she drew closer to the door, an overwhelming stench filled the air. That's when she saw something burning next to it. She stopped in her tracks. Was the house on fire? Slowly, she approached it. No, it wasn't the house. It was what appeared to be a grocery bag. But why did it smell so bad? That's when something else caught her eye. The words "Outsider. Go Home!" were spray painted on the side of the house in bright orange.

She blinked. But instead of feeling fear, she was angry. How dare someone call her an outsider! She had every right to be in this house. Grabbing her phone, she called 911. Who knew what else this person may have done?

While waiting for the police to arrive, she got in her Accord and locked the doors. Not even ten minutes later, someone drove down the long driveway, but it wasn't the police. Panic shot through her. *Had the vandals come back?!*

Chasing Her Trust

With a shaking hand, she tried to get her key into the ignition. It took several tries, but she finally made contact and started the car. She was getting ready to shift the gear when a knock at the window made her jump.

"Shit!" she shouted.

"Police. You called 911?"

She wiped away some of the condensation from the inside of the driver's window, and when an officer's badge filled her vision, she rolled it down.

"I got a call about—"

That's when she saw him. "You?"

Staring back at her were the warm mocha brown eyes of Nick Moore.

Chapter Three

The moment Nick got out of his car; he knew what type of call this would be. Even with the meager light of the moon, he could see that this huge mansion sprawled out before him was much bigger than any house his family or friends owned. He knew the type who lived in a place like this—someone who was used to others catering to their needs. He also knew that he was the newest member of the local police force, which meant he was going to get some crappy calls.

From where he stood, he could see a small fire on the front porch. He held in a laugh as he remembered how he and his buddy used to toss flaming bags of dog shit onto porches back when they were teenagers. They'd targeted anyone new to the high school. God, he'd been a little shit back then.

And here he was in a new place and hoping like hell that karma wasn't going to bite his ass.

As he approached a car parked in the driveway, it started up. He reached for his gun but stopped when he recognized the stuffed animal in the back windshield. Still, he cautiously approached the vehicle and then the blond hair came into view. He tapped the driver's window, holding his badge up.

Slowly, the glass rolled down, and even though he already knew who he was going to see, his stomach lurched when she turned her head and confirmed he was right.

"You," the familiar blond said, eyes wide.

He stepped back, cursing his luck. Of all the people in this town, it had to be the woman from the grocery store. Now that he saw where she lived, her attitude made sense.

She got out of the car and he noticed a bright pink T-shirt sticking out from beneath the Halloween sweatshirt she'd been wearing earlier. Funny fashion choice, but who was he to judge? He was lucky if he got out of the house without his tie clashing with his shirt

"Where's Harvey?" she asked him.

He growled. She wanted that asshole, Harvey? Well, maybe they deserved each other. "Busy. You got me tonight."

She rolled her eyes so hard; he was surprised they didn't lock into place.

"Look, sweetheart—"

"Don't you dare sweetheart me!" Her hands were on her hips and he was certain steam would come out of her ears if she could make it.

Most people found him intimidating, but not this woman. Hell, she looked like she was ready to throw a punch his way. But all that made him want to do was pull her into his arms and kiss her hard. He shook his head. Where the hell did that come from?

This was exactly the kind of woman he'd already learned was all wrong for him. His high school girlfriend had also come from a wealthy family and expected everyone to cater to her needs. When he'd announced he was joining the service, she'd just about had a coronary. She'd insisted he should go to college and follow in his father's footsteps.

When he'd told her his heart wasn't in business, and instead, it was important to him to join the Army, she'd said that if he did that, he wouldn't be able to provide her the lifestyle she deserved. She'd actually said those words to him.

Knowing that college wasn't for him, he'd finished out his senior year of high school, graduated, and then enlisted.

Now, here was this woman, and he had no doubt she was the same. Hell, she probably looked down on police officers. He'd never be able to afford a mansion like this. But as he stared into her eyes, he couldn't help himself. He wanted to push her buttons.

"Babe—"

"No."

"No what?"

She crossed her arms. "My name is Lauren. If you aren't going to take this seriously, I'll call Harvey."

The idea of Harvey out here alone with her made his blood boil.

"Lauren," he said as sugary sweet as he could. "Tell me what's going on."

"Follow me." She turned on her heel to approach the house, climbed the stairs, and walked across the porch, which was bigger than most people's apartments. He was curious about what might be under it.

"You coming?" Lauren asked.

He took the steps two at a time, then smelled the familiar stench. "Ah, yes. Burning dog shit."

"You know what this is? Is there someone doing this to others?"

He chuckled. "No, it's usually a high school prank. I have no idea why they would do it to you." His eyes scanned up the side of the house and saw the spray paint.

"Who's the outsider?"

Her gaze dropped to the ground as she shuffled her feet. "Me."

Well, that was unexpected. "You just buy this place or something?"

Her head jerked up, her gaze meeting his. "Or something," she said through clenched teeth.

"Well, honey, if you aren't going to be open with me, I'm afraid I can't help you." He had to hold back his grin. Five, four, three…

"If you call me some sweet name one more time, I won't care that you're an officer of the law."

There she was in his face again. Looking down into those glaring eyes of hers, he wanted her to lay hands on him. He wanted any excuse to touch her.

"Sugar." He couldn't stop his grin this time.

"That's it." She whipped out her phone. "I'm calling Harvey. At least he's a professional."

Shit. What was he doing? Flirting? God, he had no idea how to do that anymore, and besides, he was on the job.

"Harvey?"

He snatched the phone from her hand and ended the call, which he noticed was to someone named Harmony. Interesting nickname for Harvey.

"I'm sorry. You're right. I'm not being professional. That ends now, Lauren." He handed her phone back.

She bit her lip and stared at him as he waited, wondering if she was going to resume her call or work with him.

"All right," she acquiesced.

Thank fuck. He let out the breath he was holding.

She went on. "This house belonged to my stepdad. He married my mom several years ago. I only lived here when I came home during the summers of my last two years of college."

She paused and he calculated her age. She'd just come home from college? Damn, she was younger than he thought.

"So you're about twenty-two? That explains the stuffed animal in your window."

Shit. Why'd he say that? Thinking out loud was going to get him in trouble.

She tilted her head and narrowed her eyes. "No, I'm twenty-nine. Why does that matter? And is that too old to have a stuffed llama?"

He swallowed. *Yeah, Nick, why does that matter?*

"I was trying to follow the timeline you laid out about when you lived here. So you haven't lived here for about seven years?"

Good save.

"That's right. Then a few months ago, my mom and stepdad died. My stepdad's sister, Grace, was the one to call and give me the news. She told me I could stay in this house anytime I needed. Recently, my circumstances changed, and here I am. So yes, I'm technically an outsider."

The flame on the burning bag dwindled to a flicker, but the wind shifted and when the stench found them, Nick moved toward the front door, motioning to it. "Was it locked when you got here?"

She furrowed her brow. "I assumed so. I never checked."

Nick reached for the knob and tried to open it. Fortunately, it was still locked.

"Do you have any idea who would want you to leave?"

Tears welled in her eyes. "No, I don't. When I was here that last summer, everyone was so friendly. I have no idea who did this. I've been back about a month. Why now?"

Sounds like typical high school kid crap. "Probably some high school dare. I see they used orange spray paint. With Halloween coming up this week, it may have been some sad attempt to scare you. You know, a Halloween prank."

"Halloween prank? Are you serious?"

There was that glare she liked to aim his way again. And, damn, despite her privileged airs, he wanted to touch her. He shoved his hands in his pockets, needing to control himself. Here he was, new on the job and bordering on unprofessional.

"Yes. Look, the flame is out. I'm sure you're safe."

She tipped her head back to the sky and mumbled something.

"What was that?"

Her gaze locked on his. "*You're sure I'm safe?* That's the extent of your investigation?"

"If someone really wanted to hurt you, they

might have broken in or waited for you to be home to do this. Instead, this looks like something some teenager would do. I've seen it in my hometown. Hell, I've done it in my hometown. You'll be fine."

At his last job, he wouldn't have even gotten called out to something like this. They'd had real crimes to deal with there.

She mumbled something more under her breath that he didn't understand and walked to the front door. Keys jingled in the night. With one last look, she stared at him over her shoulder. Those eyes haunted him. Then the next thing he knew, the door slammed with her on the other side of it, and he was left standing alone in the dark.

He was certain it was a high school prank, but he couldn't shake the way she'd looked at him. To be safe, once he got to his car, he pulled out to the road, killed his lights, and drove partway back down her driveway. The moonlight was bright enough for him to see a clearing off to his right, so he rolled down his window to enable him to hear anyone who might come by and then killed his engine.

As he sat there listening to the crickets and an occasional frog, he shook his head. *What the hell am I doing?* Would he have done this for his old cases back home?

He closed his eyes, trying to clear his mind. That was a question he wasn't quite willing to answer yet.

Chapter Four

"Good morning! Good morning!" a familiar voice sang from inside Lauren's bedroom. "Nothing good comes from sleeping in!"

The overhead light switched on and she dove under the covers. "Ugh. What time is it?"

"Six a.m."

Lauren peeked out to spot her stepaunt, Grace, standing at the foot of her bed, all made up like she was ready for an interview.

"It's too early. I need more sleep." She loved Grace, but not at six in the morning after working last night.

"More sleep? Does this have anything to do with that man sleeping in his car in the driveway?"

Lauren shot up and ran to the window. Sure enough, Nick's car was in the driveway, but not in the same place she'd last seen it. It was now closer to the road and parked where he could easily pull out.

"That's Nick. He's a detective." She turned from the window and almost ran into Grace.

"Detective? From where? Lauren, is everything all right? What's going on?"

The memory of the burning bag came back to her, along with Nick's egotistical issues.

"When I came home last night, someone had spray-painted words on the house and there was a burning bag of dog poop by the front door."

Her aunt's hands went to her mouth. "No!"

Lauren moved past her to go back to the bed. "Wait. When did you get here? How did you miss the poop and the bright orange spray paint on the house?"

"I parked in the garage and came in through the mudroom, so I didn't see anything. What did they paint on the house?"

Lauren explained the words and how Nick had responded.

"He didn't take anything I had to say seriously, even at the store. He's some arrogant, giant of a man who thinks he knows better. I bet he's only in the driveway because he fell asleep. He told me last night it was high school kids and nothing to worry about."

Grace pursed her lips and her cheeks flushed red. "Is that so?" She snagged her phone from her pocket and it was at her ear before Lauren knew what she was doing.

"Ross, this is Grace. We need to talk."

Holy shit. Her aunt knew the police chief well enough to call him by his first name?

She must have seen the shock on Lauren's face, because she held the phone away and whispered, "We dated briefly in high school."

"Yes, I've been good. Thank you for asking. How about you?" After a pause, she spoke again, "Uh-huh. I'm calling because my niece had an incident last night. Someone named..." Her aunt turned to her. "What's his name, again?"

"Nick."

"Nick. He basically blew her off. She says he's a detective. What happened to Joey?" Grace's eyebrows shot up. "Oh, I'm sorry. I hadn't heard. But, Ross, someone spray-painted threatening words on our house and this Nick didn't take the threat seriously."

Lauren strained to hear both sides of the conversation.

"Uh-huh. Uh-huh. Thank you, Ross. I really appreciate this." Grace was smiling as she pocketed her phone. "Well, that's been taken care of." Then she eyed Lauren up and down. "I'll make breakfast. You've gotten too skinny. It's a good thing you're staying here."

She was almost to the door when Lauren found her voice. "Wait. You dated the police chief?"

Her aunt let out a chuckle and sat on the edge of the bed. "I did. I wish I'd been smart enough to hold on to that man. He's a good guy."

"I've never personally known a police chief."

"Well, this is a small town. Just about everyone knows everyone."

"I'm still getting used to that."

"That's why I want this spray paint matter to be taken seriously. If someone in this town says you aren't welcome, they need to answer to me." Grace patted her leg, then stood up.

"Grace, are you staying here too? Do you still have your house on the other side of town?"

"I do. I'm having renovations done. Well, they were supposed to do the work while I was on that cruise, but I returned yesterday, and they were just starting. I need to stay here for a little bit."

"Oh, I'm sorry about your house, but I'm glad you'll be here."

"That's good, because it looks like I'll be here through the new year. I hope that's all right."

Lauren was relieved she wouldn't be staying there by herself anymore. "That's more than all right. I don't like being in this big house alone."

Grace looked sympathetic. "I'm so sorry about what happened to Michael and your mother." Her eyes filled with tears. "They were too young."

Stretching forward, Lauren reached for her robe that was spread across the foot of her bed and wrapped it around her shoulders. "When you called to tell me they had died"—she swallowed, the words still too hard to say—"you mentioned I could stay here if I needed to."

"Yes, of course. I remember. And I'm so glad you're here."

"Well, I'm trying to save up enough to move, but it might take a little longer than I'd hoped."

Grace frowned but quickly turned it into a smile. "That's fine, dear."

"If it isn't, let me know. I'm sure I could stay with Harmony for a while."

Her aunt patted her leg. "No, it's fine. But what happened with Scott? You two were living together for quite some time."

God, she didn't want to hear his name again.

"It didn't work out."

"Do you want to talk about it?"

Lauren shook her head. "No. That's my past. This is my future. It will be nice spending time with you."

Grace clapped her hands together. "Well, let's fill this house with happy memories this holiday season. We can start by getting some Halloween decorations after breakfast."

Lauren imagined how this place would look all decorated. When it was just her and her mom, they never did anything for Halloween. Money was too tight. Plus, her mom said that if they decorated, people would knock on their door, and they didn't have any candy for them.

"Do you ever get trick-or-treaters this far out?" She was excited she might be able to give out candy.

"No, but that doesn't mean we can't get into the spirit of it all. In the meantime, I'll contact someone about removing the paint out front." Grace went to leave the room, then called over her shoulder, "Breakfast will be ready soon."

A car engine revved to life in their driveway. Lauren stood and made her way to the window just in time to watch Nick drive away.

"Ross probably chewed him out. That boy needs to learn how people treat our family in this town," Grace said as she glared out the window.

As much as Lauren enjoyed spending time with Grace, she'd forgotten her aunt was used to everyone catering to her needs. While Lauren wanted to make sure Nick didn't treat anyone else the way he'd treated her, she also didn't expect special treatment.

"You might want to get dressed. Ross said he'd stop by this morning."

"You didn't need to ask him to do that."

Her aunt cocked her head. "You heard me on the phone. I didn't." She grinned. "Ross still has a thing for me. Whenever I'm in town, he makes a point of stopping by." Then she winked.

Lauren suppressed her laugh. The image of

her aunt and the police chief was not one she wanted in her mind. Although it'd probably be good for the chief. According to Harmony, ever since his wife passed away several years ago, he'd closed himself off to everyone. Lauren had heard that was when his son, Joey, began to have problems. She didn't understand at the time how crushing grief could be. But now, missing her mom every day, she understood.

Grief could make people do things they wouldn't normally do.

Chapter Five

Nick's neck cracked as he turned his head. Apparently, it had been too long since he'd done a stakeout. He'd lasted maybe an hour outside Lauren's house before he'd fallen asleep. Then he was rudely awakened by a call from his new boss, chewing his ass out for the way he'd handled the situation with Lauren. Little did Chief Dunin know, he'd been parked outside her place all night.

The heavy door to the police station opened as Harvey walked out, staring at his phone. Nick stepped to the side to avoid being trampled, but Harvey must have sensed his presence, because he glanced up and a grin broke out across his face.

"Boss is waiting for you. And he's livid!" Harvey singsonged as he practically skipped away.

Before facing his new boss, Nick needed

caffeine, so he made his way to the kitchenette and grabbed a cup of coffee.

"Moore! My office. Now!"

He guzzled as much coffee as he could as he followed the chief into his office.

"Shut the door."

As he did so, he spotted a large, furry fake spider attached to the wall.

"You like spiders, sir?" Nick asked, gesturing toward it. Then he noticed a number of Halloween decorations around the office.

The anger melted from the chief's face as he glanced at the spider in question. "I like Halloween. But that's not why I asked you in here. Sit down!" he barked out.

Nick sat, choosing the chair closest to the door.

"What the hell were you thinking blowing off someone in the Chanler family?"

"The Chanler family? Her name is Lauren Chanler?" Saying it brought a smile to his lips, but he forced a frown. Nothing about her should cause him to smile.

"No, it's Lauren Harrow."

He cocked his head. "Not Chanler. So I didn't blow off a Chanler."

The chief ran his hand over his beard as he mumbled something under his breath. Then he stood and came around the desk. "You admit you blew her off?"

Nick's brows shot up. "No! I didn't blow her off. I did my job."

"Look, I realize you're new to town and don't have the benefit of knowing the history I do, so let me fill you in. That big mansion you went to last night? That belongs to the Chanler family. That family has done more for this town than anyone. Hell, they single-handedly fund the summer camp for kids. If they need our help, you give it to them. You understand?"

Nick knew how small towns ran. He also knew he was the outsider, so if this would help move things along, he could do that. "Understood. They get special treatment."

The chief slammed his fist on his desk. "Goddammit. No, not special treatment. Respect." He walked around to his chair. "That woman you blew off last night was Mr. Chanler's stepdaughter."

"Did she actually tell you I blew her off?" The early call was coming back to haunt him. He'd been asleep when the chief phoned but had tried to sound as awake as possible. The princess must have complained about him. Guess she was used to everyone giving her what she wanted. He couldn't swallow down the grin at imagining her fuming because he hadn't done what she expected.

"No, that's what a very angry Grace said when we spoke."

"Who's Grace?" Lauren couldn't even contact

the chief herself? She had to get someone else to. Wow, that woman was a piece of work.

"Grace was Mr. Chanler's sister."

"Was?"

"Mr. Chanler passed away a few months ago. But that doesn't change anything. That family deserves our respect."

Nick let out a sigh. "I didn't brush her off. I remained parked outside her home all night. When you called this morning, that's where I was."

"Really? Because when you answered, you sounded like you'd just woken up. Need some skills training in staying awake?"

Nick grumbled, "No."

"You look like hell. Take the morning off. Go shower or something." Dunin grabbed a pen and focused on the paperwork in front of him, effectively dismissing Nick, who took that opportunity to leave. And, fortunately, Harvey hadn't returned, so he didn't have to deal with his sorry ass on his way out of the station.

Once Nick was back on the street, the aroma of bacon wafted in the air and his stomach growled. Food first, then a shower. But he'd rather not take another shower in his motel room. He had to find somewhere with better water pressure soon.

Of course, the motel was temporary. He was looking for an apartment, but everywhere he'd inquired, he'd been told the unit was no longer available.

    Maybe Harvey was right, and no one wanted him here. Maybe others here felt he was as temporary as he felt. If he had to stay at the motel, so be it. He figured that after six months, he could apply to go back to his old job. Surely the sheriff there wouldn't still be angry with him by then. Nick had been closed-minded. He could admit that. But in the end, the case had been resolved. It had all worked out.

    After walking a few blocks, he found the source of the heavenly bacon scent. Lucky's Diner. From the outside, it resembled a fifties diner.

    As he stepped inside, he noticed an old jukebox in the corner. Booths lined the windows, and the counter had several retro style stools. All the upholstery was red vinyl, which felt right. There were fake spiderwebs framing the windows with spiders thrown in here and there.

    Spotting an open stool, he sat down and grabbed a menu from the counter. It listed the usual diner fare.

    "Looks like it's safe to return to the station now." Nick heard the familiar voice and turned to his right to find Harvey sitting a couple of seats over, drinking a cup of coffee.

    "Did you get fired yet?" Harvey asked.

    Nick grunted. "I'm afraid you're out of luck."

    Harvey set his cup down and stood. "Damn. I think I'm out of the pool."

"The pool?"

"Yep, we all bet on when you'd get fired. There were a lot of takers for that bet. Have a nice day, Moore." Harvey tilted his head and moved toward the door. "See you later, Harmony!" he shouted before he left.

"Bye!" a woman called out as she walked up to Nick.

"Hey, hon. Can I get you some coffee?"

Nick's gaze took in her outfit. She was decked out in jeans and a pink T-shirt that was brighter than Pepto-Bismol. What was it with bright pink in this town? His mind immediately went to Lauren and the bit of pink he'd seen poking out from under her sweatshirt.

"Oh, hey. You're new." A broad smile spread across her face.

He knew that look. She had long red hair pulled into a ponytail and big brown eyes. She was cute in a wholesome way but not his type. Her nametag read "Harmony."

"Hey, Harmony. I'm the new detective."

Her eyes widened. Yep, word had gotten around.

"Nick?" she asked.

He cocked his head. Word really had gotten around. "Yes."

The waitress crossed her arms and her lips thinned into a straight line. "Well, Nick, Mr.

Detective. I'll have you know that Lauren is my best friend and I heard you haven't treated her very well."

This was interesting. "Is that so?" He spun around on the stool so that he was fully facing the woman.

"Yes, and if you don't want me spitting in your food, you're going to apologize to her today."

He leaned back on the stool, elbows resting on the counter behind him. "I will? Now how will you know if I've done that?"

The waitress smirked. "Because I'll watch you do it. Lauren's due in any minute."

Great. Maybe he should take his order to go.

"All right then. While we wait, can I order?" If he hurried, he could get his food and be out of there before Lauren showed up.

The redhead glared at him. "What do you want?"

"I'll take your breakfast special," he told her, and when she continued to glare at him, he couldn't resist adding, "To go."

Now she raised a brow. "I'll put that in for you, but I'm not serving you until after the apology."

Guess she saw through his plan. He couldn't help but grin.

But that grin fell off his face when Lauren walked in the front door of the diner wearing the same pink T-shirt with jeans uniform his waitress wore.

"Wait, Lauren's a waitress?"

The woman looked over her shoulder then back at him. Her hands went to her hips. "Is that a problem?"

He frowned. *Why would she be working as a waitress?*

"I've been to her house. She doesn't need money. Why would she work here?"

Then he remembered a buddy in high school who was an actor that played a postal worker. He went to the post office and interviewed actual postal workers on their jobs.

"Is she an actress?" He couldn't take his eyes off her as she walked to the rear of the restaurant and out of sight. When his gaze fell back to Harmony, she was chuckling.

"What?"

"You think Lauren is an actress after watching her walk in here wearing a pink T-shirt that matches mine? And you're a detective?" The woman bent over laughing. "Rumor has it, you were booted from the county sheriff's office. I think I know why."

She spun on her heel, and as she walked away, she said, "Wait till Lauren hears this." She snickered and retreated from the dining room.

He sat there, stunned, as he ran through the possibilities in his mind. Why would she work here when she's rich? His boss said she was the stepdaughter. Maybe she doesn't have any of the

Chanler money. No, that wasn't possible. The way she behaved around him and then having her aunt call his boss—she was a privileged princess. He was sure of it. But he'd also been sure about Josh Morgan on his last case, and not only had that blown up in his face, it was the reason he was now stuck in Fisher Springs.

Is it possible he misjudged Lauren and she's not some sort of rich, entitled snob? No. It's more likely she already blew through her inheritance. That made more sense. He had a cousin who did that. He also had that same entitled attitude.

The kind of attitude that leads to someone throwing a burning bag of shit on your porch.

He chuckled at the thought.

Twenty minutes later, he sat there, still without food or Lauren. He was growing hungrier by the minute. Finally, a new waitress came out carrying a bag and headed in his direction.

"Here you go sir, breakfast special. Is there anything else I can get you?"

Now he was certain Lauren was avoiding him.

"Yes, can you tell me a little about Lauren?"

The woman's face lit up. "Sure can. She's a sweet little thing." Then a nervous expression crossed her features and she took a step back. "Wait. Are you some kind of creeper?"

He showed her his badge. "No, it's for a case I'm investigating."

She frowned. "Is Lauren in trouble?"

He had to pull out the big guns here. He flashed his smile and turned up the charm. "No, not at all. I'm investigating what appears to be a prank pulled on her, but I need some background information about her in order to fully understand why she was targeted. You know, does she work here? Has she always lived in the Chanler mansion?"

The woman cocked her head. "Did you ask her directly?"

Damn, his charm wasn't working. His smile widened. He'd been told he had irresistible dimples. "I haven't had the chance. Tell me, is there anyone in town who would want to scare her off?"

"Kate! Orders are piling up!" a robust man with his hands on his hips yelled in her direction.

"My boss. Gotta go."

And there went his source for information. Nick stared at the bag of food, wishing he hadn't asked for it to go. But, actually, there was no reason to go. He pulled the container out and opened the lid. Pancakes, eggs, bacon, and hash browns. His stomach growled as he grabbed a fork and dug in.

"What do you want to know about the Chanlers?"

Nick's gaze met the man to his right, who was now occupying the seat Harvey had vacated. The man appeared to be around thirty and had brown hair that looked like he just woke up. His beard, however, was neatly trimmed. He was wearing a dress shirt with the sleeves pushed up on arms that were inked all the way to his wrists.

"Zach Brannigan." He held out his hand.

"Nick," Nick said as he shook it. "Do you know Lauren? Apparently, she works here."

"Yeah, the blond? I wish I knew her better, if you know what I mean." Zach smirked and gave Nick a wink.

Nick wanted to punch the smarmy look right off his face.

Wait. Why?

"She came into my bar once. I own the pub up the street. I tried flirting with her, but then I found out she was dating Scott Fisher, so I backed down. That's one family you don't want to piss off."

"Why is that?" Nick asked as he ignored his disappointment that she had a boyfriend. Although he obviously wasn't a good one since he didn't come over after the prank.

"The Fishers? Are you serious?"

Nick shrugged. "Yeah. Why are they so special?"

The man stared at him, holding a bite of food that hadn't quite made it to his mouth yet, then informed Nick, "This is Fisher Springs. The Fisher family founded it."

It took considerable effort to hold back the eye roll that was working its way through Nick's mind.

Chasing Her Trust

"So any person with that last name is feared?"

"Feared? No. But everyone loves Scott. As a business owner in this town, I try not to piss people off. Taking Scott's girl? That would do it."

Lauren's boyfriend is likely also a self-entitled prick.

Zach added, "I was surprised when I found her working here last week. Figured she'd be living rich on whatever money stepdaddy Chanler left her."

"What happened to Mr. Chanler?"

"Mr. Chanler and Lauren's mom died while on vacation a few months ago. The whole town was pretty torn up about it."

Nick glanced toward the door again. Still no sign of her. She was avoiding him.

Zach patted his arm. "I gotta go. If you ever want a beer, come check out my bar. It's a few doors down."

"Thank you. I will."

After another twenty minutes had passed, Nick gave up on seeing Lauren, so he left the diner. On his way back to his car, his phone buzzed in his pocket.

"Detective Moore," he answered.

"I know I told you to take the morning off, but your chance to redeem yourself just came in," the chief boomed in his ear.

Great, so much for catching up on sleep.

Dunin continued. "Lauren just called from the

Chanler mansion. Sounds like someone ransacked the place."

She snuck out the back of the diner? What the hell? She wanted to avoid him that much?

"You need to get over there. Remember to be thorough. Moore, I'm giving you a second chance here."

"I'm on my way," he said through gritted teeth. He pocketed his phone and got in his car. A smile spread across his face when he imagined Lauren's expression when she saw him.

Chapter Six

Lauren rocked back and forth on the top front porch step, trembling. It was almost a cliché since it was Halloween. When she'd arrived home, the front door had been ajar. Assuming her aunt had left it open, Lauren had called for her. Then she'd seen the broken mirror and the box of files dumped on the floor.

Terrified, she'd run outside and called the police. At least she knew Nick was off duty. Hopefully, Harvey would arrive soon. That was one benefit of befriending Harmony—Lauren got her best friend, Harvey, as a friend too.

A coyote howled in the distance and she startled. As she waited, she wondered if whoever had done this was watching her.

No, they had to have left. If anyone had still been nearby, they would have heard her call for the police.

A vehicle slowly came down the long driveway. It wasn't a patrol car. Lauren jumped down the steps of the porch and ran out into the yard. Perched behind a nearby tree, she kept her eyes on the familiar car as it approached and parked. Where had she seen it before?

Then Nick got out.

"Shit," Lauren said, louder than she intended.

Nick froze. "Who's there?"

Well, she couldn't hide from him forever.

"Lauren." She moved away from the tree.

Nick's hands went to his hips. "Trying to avoid me again?" His lip hitched up for just a second before his expression turned serious.

"I'm not avoiding you." She hugged herself tightly.

"Are you shivering?"

Before she could stop him, he had his jacket off and around her shoulders.

"Thank you. I'm a little shaken up. Someone broke in."

His arms went around her, pulling her close. And the next thing Lauren knew, her cheek was pressed against his very muscular chest and her nostrils were filled with his cologne. Her body tingled from his touch. Despite her mind knowing she shouldn't like him; all her girly parts didn't get the memo. He had the tall, dark, and handsome thing going on, and at the moment, she was worn out, so instead of fighting him, she melted into him and accepted his comfort. But why was he being so nice to her, especially after her aunt called and got him chewed out?

Ah. Now she understood—this was all about Grace knowing the chief. Lauren pulled away from him. "Don't do this."

Nick quirked a brow. "Do what?"

"Be nice. This isn't you."

He threw his head back and laughter filled the air. "How the hell would you know what *is* me?"

Lauren crossed her arms. "Really? You haven't been nice to me yet. And you don't need to be fake polite. Just catch whoever broke in."

He copied her stance, crossing his arms as well. "I will, but I need to check the place out first. Tell me what you saw when you arrived home."

All she could focus on was the way his arms flexed when he crossed them. How had she not noticed how muscular he was before?

"Can you answer the question?"

Oh shit. Did he ask a question?

When she dared to glance up, his smoldering gaze met hers. Then he took a couple of steps forward and they were almost toe-to-toe, much too close for strangers.

"Sorry to distract you. Perhaps now you can concentrate on my words." He winked.

And the real Nick was back.

"You smug ass—"

"Hey, before you go around insulting me, don't you want me to investigate, princess?"

To keep from wiping the arrogant look off his face, she spun around and walked up the stairs. At the top, she turned to him. "Will this be as thorough as your last investigation, Detective?"

His jaw clenched as he glared at her. Then he was on the porch and in her space again, and as much as she wanted to take a step back, she wouldn't give him the satisfaction.

"What happened when you arrived home?"

Holding her ground, she lifted her chin, her eyes meeting his. "I got to the front door and noticed it was ajar. I assumed that maybe Grace had left it open. But when I went inside, I saw a broken mirror and papers everywhere."

"Who's Grace?"

"My aunt."

"Anyone else live here?"

"No, it's only the two of us right now."

"Stay here. I'm going to have a look around."

Without waiting for her response, Nick left her on the porch and went into the house. The coyotes howled from the green belt again, spooking her, so she ignored his instructions and followed him into the house.

He stopped and held his hand up. "I said to

wait here. I don't want you tampering with my crime scene."

"Crime scene?" she hissed. "This is where I live."

He quirked a brow. "Must you argue with everything I say?"

She crossed her arms and glared. "I'm not arguing."

He chuckled. "Always have to get the last word in too, I see." He turned and went past the entry room with the broken mirror.

"No, I don't," she called out, just loud enough to make sure he heard her.

He shook his head as he continued toward the back of the house. Then he rounded a corner and she lost sight of him.

Standing alone in the entryway, she felt vulnerable, so she tiptoed after him. Once she rounded the same corner, she came to a halt in the doorway of the room that had been her stepdad's office. High up on the wall, someone had spray-painted the words "Outsider" and "Go Home."

This was directed at her. Grace lived in this town. She was from here. Lauren had only returned because she had nowhere else to go. She was the outsider and someone wanted her to leave.

Her mind raced. She'd heard that Scott was back in town. Maybe his assistant came with him and wanted her out of the picture. She shook her head.

No, why would she do that? Lauren had left Scott the moment she found out. She was no threat to the assistant.

"You don't take instruction well, do you?" Nick was there, in her space again, and any warmth she thought she'd seen in his eyes earlier was gone.

"Sorry, I just didn't want to be alone."

Alone. Suddenly, she missed her mother as another wave of grief overtook her. Damn it. She had no control over her emotions lately. She turned away, hoping he didn't see the tears welling in her eyes.

He sighed behind her. "No, I'm sorry. I've been an ass."

She shrugged her shoulders. She wanted to scream *Hell yeah, you have!* But that probably wouldn't help things.

"Do you have any idea who would do this?" Nick asked.

She needed to focus on Nick and not her grief or the spray-painted wall. Taking a deep breath, she calmed herself as she wiped away her tears, and then she faced him again. "No."

He gave a quick nod of his head. "Well, the ransacking was one thing, but this is personal. It appears to be targeting you."

She nodded in agreement. What else could she say?

He reached out and put his hands on her shoulders. Heat radiated throughout her body from his touch. She averted her gaze to hide her reaction.

"I need you to wait here while I look at the rest of the house. All right?"

Damn it. He was being nice Nick again. She really liked nice Nick. She simply tipped her head and he left the room.

She fell to her knees, her thoughts sifting through who could have done this. She'd never felt like an outsider in this town. All the people here had been so welcoming since that first summer she'd come home from college. Her stepdad had made a point to introduce her around town and he let everyone know she was now his family. *His family.* Regret washed over her for not visiting more.

Heavy footsteps on the stairs made her stand tall, but she relaxed slightly when she realized it was Nick.

"I've checked all the rooms. It looks like the damage is confined to downstairs. No one is in the house. I'll need to collect some evidence. It shouldn't take long, and then you can get back to whatever you planned to do today."

What? He was going to leave her here in this house? Alone? After what just happened? Someone could be waiting in the trees along the green belt until he left. And if they were, no one would notice. It was Halloween. Anyone could hide in the shadows tonight.

"That's it?" she snapped.

He frowned. "What do you mean?"

"That's the extent of your investigation? You're going to leave? This isn't some prank." The more she realized that that was his intent, the angrier she became.

"Please call the police chief and ask him to come out here. At least he knows how to fully investigate," she said. Her hands were now on her hips.

His eyes narrowed as he moved closer to her. "This isn't some big city. And this isn't a murder. There's no CSI team to bring in. You want to call him again and tell him I'm not doing my job?" He reached into his pocket. "Use my phone." He held it out to her.

She took a step back, and he smirked.

"That's right, your aunt called last time. You wouldn't dare get your fingers dirty and do something yourself? Damn. You are a princess."

He turned on his heel and headed for the front door.

"A princess?" She was right behind him. "That's better than some arrogant city cop who thinks he knows better than everyone else."

Nick stopped suddenly, so suddenly that she ran into him.

He spun around. "I'm not a city cop. I'm a detective—"

"And I'm not a princess. I'm not even rich. I'm only staying here because I have nowhere else to go!"

Why the hell was she telling him this?

His gaze took in the mansion. "You're not rich?" He chuckled. "Okay."

She rolled her eyes. "For a detective, you're pretty dense. My mom married Mr. Chanler. That gives me the right to stay here, but that's it."

Nick cocked his head. "You're not a trust fund kid?"

She laughed. "No. My mom was a single mom and did the best she could. After I went to college, on student loans, by the way, she met Mr. Chanler and married him. I certainly never got the benefit of"—she spun around—"all this."

He held her gaze. "I'm sorry I misjudged you." His mocha eyes looked sincere. "I realize you aren't comfortable staying here, and like you said, you don't have anywhere else to go."

He scratched the back of his neck. "Can you call your boyfriend to come over?"

She crossed her arms. "Boyfriend?"

"Yeah, aren't you dating the founder's son or some shit like that?" He shifted from one foot to the other.

"You asked about me?" She grinned. The big, bad detective asked about her?

He frowned. "No, when I was at the diner earlier and you were avoiding me—"

"I was not avoiding you!"

"It doesn't matter. But the guy next to me

heard me asking the waitress about you—"

"You admit you asked about me." Her grin got wider.

"Yeah, I asked where the hell you were since I was sitting there waiting to apologize."

"You really wanted to apologize?"

"No, I really wanted my breakfast. Harmony was holding it hostage until I apologized. Anyway, if you'll let me finish, the guy next to me overheard me asking about you and he was eager to fill me in."

"Who was this guy?"

"Zach Brannigan. He said he owns a pub."

"Oh. Yeah. But he's wrong. I'm not with Scott anymore." She swallowed her disappointment. Of course Nick wasn't asking about her relationship status. Why would he? They clearly didn't like each other.

"Well, in that case, since it's Halloween, I'm guessing people will be coming to the door and it's probably best you aren't alone. I can stay here and keep an eye on the place."

Her thoughts were spinning. "Wait. Stay here?"

He shrugged. "Just for the night. Maybe we'll get lucky and catch the perp tomorrow. Besides, I'm staying in a motel that isn't that great. This would be a step up."

There was an extra bedroom that he could use, and having someone here would make her feel better.

She wasn't even sure if her aunt was staying here tonight or not.

"You really think you'll catch whoever did this tomorrow?"

He smiled. "Nope. But we can take each day as it comes. After I collect some evidence, I'm going to head back to the station for a while. Then I'll run to the motel and get my things."

She nodded. "All right. You have a deal." Although, damn it, she would still be alone for a while. She could do this, though.

She extended her hand and he shook it. Again, his touch lit her up.

He started through the door, then turned around. "What's your phone number?"

"My number?" Her stomach fluttered. Was he really asking for her number?

"Yeah, then I'll call you so that you'll have mine. You know, in case anything else comes up before I get back."

She gave him her number and after he left and she'd locked up, she leaned against the door and slid down it with a smile.

Someone was trying to scare her out of town and all she could think about was Nick. The infuriating, arrogant, sexy as hell detective.

Maybe Harmony had it right. He could make a good rebound guy. And the fact that she didn't really like him would keep her heart safe.

Chapter Seven

By the time Nick returned to the mansion, it was late. He'd gone out on a call involving some man trying to put a costume on another man's horse. Turns out, it involved too much alcohol and a dare, and it ended up taking longer than it should have.

With his bag in his hand, he knocked on the door. She hadn't called or texted him, so maybe that meant she'd relaxed since he left.

Lauren answered, holding a glass of wine. Instead of the hideously bright pink T-shirt, she was wearing a formfitting fuzzy blue sweater and tight black pants. His eyes slowly raked up her body, taking in all her curves. He may have let out a small groan, because when his gaze met hers, she grinned.

"You came back." She seemed happy to see him.

Nick returned her smile. "Sorry, I had to answer a call that took longer than it should have."

"I'm glad you're here now." She opened the door further to allow him to enter. "This way."

Instead of going up the stairs, she headed toward the back of the house. He followed.

"Would you like a glass of wine?" she asked him.

"No, I should stay alert."

She nodded. "Right. Well, I've had a long day and—"

"You don't need to explain anything to me."

She led him into a room that had a large gray wraparound couch that was positioned in front of a very large television.

"I've got a horror movie cued up if you want to watch."

"You want to watch horror?" He didn't even try to hide his surprise. "I'm not sure that's a good idea. You were pretty scared earlier."

She took a large sip of her wine, then sat down on the couch. "I was. But it's Halloween and this is sort of a tradition of mine. What about you? What would you be doing if you weren't here?"

He laughed. "I'd be sitting in a sad motel room. Do you do anything else besides watch a horror flick?"

A smile spread across her face. "Nope." She grabbed the bottle from the coffee table and poured more wine into her glass.

He dropped his bag on the floor and took a seat on the opposite end of the couch. Despite trying to keep his gaze on anything but her, he couldn't help but notice her black bra strap where her sweater fell off her shoulder. He imagined it was black lace. The clothes she was wearing did nothing to hide her curves. Her hair was down and, damn, he couldn't stop his body from reacting to her. Hopefully she wouldn't notice. He shifted his focus back to the television. A horror movie should kill any thoughts he had of Lauren naked. Or of Lauren's mouth on him. He lunged for the remote on the table. Time to get this movie started.

"All right. Let's watch this." He turned it on.

As the movie played, the reality of his situation settled in. One moment, he couldn't stand this woman, yet after a few words, he'd agreed to spend the night here. And what was he going to tell the chief? He'd already filled him in on the ransacking. But his staying there was something else. There's no way this was proper protocol. Lauren was hot, there was no denying that. And that was why the chief was going to misread his intentions.

Hell, what *were* his intentions? Five years as a detective and he'd never offered to spend the night at a crime victim's home. He'd stayed in his car and watched before. From outside. But, damn. She was in this huge house all alone. What else could he do? It was Halloween, which was creepy in itself. Then the fact there were two incidences and both involved spray-painted words on the walls. This time, it was inside, though. He needed to get the handwriting analyzed to determine if it was the same person. This was a pretty minor case and would be low on the county's priority list, but maybe his connections would help.

He had to tell Chief Dunin he was staying here. "I'll be right back. Keep playing the movie."

Lauren nodded while taking another sip of wine.

He stepped out onto the front porch. No sign of any trick-or-treaters and none had knocked while he'd been there. Guess this house was too far away from everything.

While he dialed, he ran over what he planned to say in his head. Yep, this wasn't going to go well.

"Chief Dunin."

"It's Moore. I'm back at the Chanler house."

"Did something else happen?"

"No. I told Lauren I'd keep an eye out in case anyone returns."

"Are you camped out in your car again? Last time you did that, you looked like crap and were worthless at work."

He shoved his free hand into his pocket and took a deep breath.

"Actually, I'm staying in the house."

"Shit, Moore. She's a victim of a crime, not some hookup. I swear to God, if you—"

"No, it's not like that. I'm staying in an extra room so I can watch the place. It's a mansion. There are a lot of extra bedrooms."

The chief sighed into the phone. "You remember she's a victim in an ongoing investigation. She's off limits!"

Nick held the phone out while Dunin yelled.

"Chief, you have nothing to worry about. I'm not going to risk an investigation. Besides, she's not my type. I don't go for privileged princesses." He cringed as soon as the words were out of his mouth. Lauren had already corrected his judgmental attitude toward her.

"What? Where'd you get that impression? You know what, never mind. Just keep your hands to yourself. We'll talk tomorrow." The chief ended the call.

Back in the living room, Lauren was intently watching the movie credits. "You missed the ending."

He chuckled. "I'm sure I could guess how it ended."

She looked at him and smiled. "Yeah, it was pretty predictable, wasn't it?"

Nick yawned. "I should probably get some rest." He was still exhausted from sleeping in his car the night before. "Which bedroom am I using?"

Her eyes roamed up his legs and slowly took

in his body. Damn, she wasn't even trying to hide it.

"Are you drunk?" He regretted the words the moment they came out of his mouth.

Her faced flushed red and she walked past him. "No. Follow me and I'll show you your room."

He trailed her upstairs. "It's all right if you are. Understandable, actually. But I just want to know which version of you was checking me out down there."

She stopped suddenly and he nearly ran into her. She motioned into the room. "You can stay in here. There's a shared bathroom between this room and mine. But make sure to lock both doors if you use it." Then she spun around to face him. "And I wasn't checking you out."

He arched a brow.

"All right. Maybe I was. But only because you'd changed clothes from earlier. I was curious as to why."

Instead of his usual suit he wore for work, he'd put on a T-shirt and jeans. Hell, he could probably wear that for work in this town. Everyone was so casual.

"This is my after-work uniform."

"Uniform?"

"Yeah."

He walked into the bedroom and she stood in the doorway. When his eyes met the far wall, he stopped short. A muffled chuckle came from Lauren.

"Sorry." She wore a full grin.

He looked back at the wall, which was like a page from one of his nightmares. It was covered with dolls. Not just regular dolls but creepy ass dolls. There had to be five shelves of them that lined the entire expanse of the wall, and there wasn't any free space to fit even one more.

Lauren laughed. "The expression on your face right now. It's priceless."

He eyed her. "Why do you have such creepy dolls? And why so many? Are you a secret psychopath? Shit, was that horror movie a set-up so I wouldn't suspect you?"

She patted his arm and, damn, it felt good. "You'll be safe in here, Detective." She laughed some more. "My aunt collects dolls. I don't know why they ended up here and not at her house. I agree, they *are* creepy as hell. Hopefully, they won't keep you up at night."

His gaze met hers. Was she messing with him? Is that why he was in the doll room? Then another thought hit him. "Your room is on the other side of this wall?"

"Yes."

He quirked a brow.

"Trust me, I wanted to put you on a different floor, but this is the only other room with a bed in it."

When he checked this floor after the ransacking, he noticed at least two other bedrooms with beds. Funny, she was putting him next to her. "What's in the other ones?"

"Well, there are actually two more with beds. But my stepbrother, William, claimed the master. Then my stepaunt, Grace, claimed the other one. They both have quite a bit of their belongings here. The rest were used as hobby rooms by my mom and Michael. One is for sewing, another for a miniature town."

"Anyone else going to be staying here?"

She shook her head. "No. Well, Grace was here last night, but she called to say she wouldn't be here tonight. William lives in Portland and only comes home for July fourth celebrations."

"All right. I'll make sure everything is locked up and then I'm going to bed."

She nodded. "I'm going to read a bit before I go to sleep. I'll see you in the morning, Detective."

He turned to say goodnight but noticed her eyes on his chest again. He crossed his arms, purposely flexing his muscles. When her gaze traveled upward and met his, he couldn't help but smile. Her cheeks became rosy as she spun on her heel and left.

She liked the way he looked and that made him feel a lot better than it should have.

After he checked all the locks, he returned to his room and stripped down to his boxer briefs before sliding between the sheets. He switched off the lamp, and the moonlight that streamed through the curtainless window made the room lighter than he normally cared for.

With his back to the window, he closed his eyes in frustration, but then he heard a buzzing sound. Light he could deal with but not noise too. He walked toward it, and it grew louder as he got closer to the dolls. The damn things were buzzing? No, it was coming from the other side of the wall. He put his ear to it after he managed to find a small open space. A faint moan accompanied the buzzing sound.

Holy shit. *Could it be?* Another moan. Was Lauren masturbating? The thought of her pressing a vibrator between her legs had him instantly hard. No, he should get back in that bed and pretend he never heard anything. But he didn't. He couldn't pull himself away from the wall. Then she let out a scream that was quickly muffled and the buzzing ended. His heart was beating fast and he suddenly wanted to relieve the ache she'd caused.

Had she wanted him to hear her? Did she do that every night? Thoughts of Lauren writhing beneath him as he pounded into her flooded his brain. He shook them away. No, he was there to protect her, as a detective. He had to focus.

When Nick's door to the bathroom clicked shut quietly, he realized she was in there. He started for it, but when he glanced down and saw that his erection was obvious in his underwear, he threw on his jeans then headed toward it again.

What the hell am I doing?

Before he could figure that out, the door opened and there was Lauren, wearing one of the sexiest, skimpiest nightgowns he'd ever seen.

"Nick!" She jumped back. "I thought you were downstairs checking on everything."

Oh, this was too much fun.

"I was. It didn't take very long."

Her brow furrowed. "Oh? You've been up here for a while then?"

He leaned against the doorframe and shoved his hands in his front pockets. "Only long enough to hear moaning and a vibrating sound coming from your room."

He'd never seen a woman flush as red as Lauren did in that instant.

Leaning down, he whispered into her ear. "What were you doing, Lauren?"

Her eyes widened. "What? Oh. That was probably my automatic pencil sharpener you heard."

"Automatic pencil sharpener?" He could barely contain his laughter.

She stood taller. "Yes, I like to write. It relaxes me."

Now his cheeks were hurting from grinning so big. "I bet it does."

"Well, goodnight." She turned and went into her bedroom.

He called out, "Well, if you run out of batteries

for your *pencil sharpener*, let me know. I have something that could help you out."

"Never going to happen, Detective." She was in the adjoining bathroom again. His gaze traveled over her body, and with the bright light on, he could almost see through her little nightgown. "And I *was* using a pencil sharpener!" She slammed the door as she went back into her room.

He chuckled. God, he loved riling her up.

Chapter Eight

Lauren was gasping for air as she jogged up the final hill of the driveway. Why did she think jogging after inhaling a bottle of wine and who knows how much candy on Halloween was a good idea?

Oh yeah, because she'd tossed and turned half the night after her encounter with Nick. She was so embarrassed that she decided running from Nick was a better choice than possibly running into whoever had ransacked the house. And instead of the run clearing her head, she felt like she'd run into a wall while all she did was think about that infuriating man. He was the type of arrogant, controlling man that she'd just been in a relationship with. Men like him—like Scott—all they wanted was their ego stroked. And if you didn't do it for them, they'd find someone else who would. No thank you.

It didn't matter that Nick was insanely sexy or…those abs. Why wasn't he wearing a shirt last night? No. That didn't matter.

It had simply been too long since she'd had sex. Things with Scott had cooled down so much in their last few months together. She made a mental note to go out with Harmony. Maybe she could find someone, just for a night.

Anything to get her mind off Nick.

When she entered the house, it was quiet. She tiptoed upstairs. Nick's door was still closed. Good, she really didn't want to face him all sweaty post-run. She needed to get cleaned up before he started whatever his morning routine was.

After taking a hot shower, where she might have used up all the hot water—*sorry, not sorry, Nick*—the doorbell rang. She glanced at her phone sitting on the bathroom counter. Ten after seven. Who the hell would be here this early? The doorbell chimed three more times. She ran into her room and quickly put her nightgown back on. Then she caught a glimpse of herself in the mirror.

Crap! She wore this in front of Nick last night? But after she thought about it, she grinned. Maybe it gave him a taste of his own medicine.

She tossed on her robe as she heard the bell again. Someone was about to catch some fresh hell. Throwing open the door to her bedroom, she ran into Nick coming out of his.

He was still shirtless and in boxer briefs and was squinting like he was half-asleep, which he must have been not to notice the hard wood he was sporting. And, boy, was he sporting it. No wonder he was so arrogant. Apparently, he had the balls to back it up.

"Can you tell your friend to text you next time? Who rings the doorbell at this time of morning?"

Lauren growled. It was too early to deal with Nick.

"First, I have no idea who the hell it is, but they're about to get an earful. Second, uh...that." She waved her finger around.

He scrunched up his face. "What the hell are you talking about?"

She pointed to his crotch. "That thing. Put it away."

He threw his head back and laughed. "Well, tell you what. You agree to not walk around in a see-through gown at night and I'll agree to put on pants before I leave the room. Deal?"

The doorbell rang several more times. Deal? Was he staying more than one night? And why did that idea excite her?

"Fine. Now can you move? I need to go yell at someone."

He shook his head. "Let me go ahead of you. To be safe." Then he started for the stairs.

"Seriously? You aren't going to holster that

thing first?"

He laughed as he turned and went into his room. A minute later, he came out, buttoning up his jeans.

She stayed close on his heels down the stairs and to the front door. When he opened it, two men stood there, looking more than annoyed.

"Can I help you?" Nick asked.

"Finally," one of them grumbled. "We have a delivery for William Chanler."

Lauren moved in front of Nick. "He's not here. He doesn't live here. I don't know when I'll see him again."

Mr. Grumpy frowned at her while the taller of the two men scanned a clipboard he was holding. The tall man pointed to the clipboard. "Mr. Chanler sent this to himself."

"I don't know why. As I said, he doesn't live here."

The man's gaze moved from the clipboard to Lauren. "Look, we're already behind schedule. We just need to know where to put these boxes. The rest, you can take up with Mr. Chanler."

Nick put his hand on her shoulder. "Sure, can you put them in the corner of that room?" He pointed to the living room right off the entry. "How many boxes?"

"Ten," Grumpy said as they headed back to their large moving truck.

"Ten? What the hell's in them?" Lauren shouted to them.

"No idea," the same one answered. They used a dolly to wheel in several boxes at a time. As soon as the last one was deposited in the living room, the man with the clipboard handed Lauren a pen. "Please sign here to confirm that the boxes were delivered."

She signed, now wanting the men to leave so she could see what her dear stepbrother had sent over.

"You weren't expecting this?" Nick asked as she stared at the boxes.

"No."

"You said he has a room upstairs but doesn't live here, right?"

"That's right. He visits once a year in the summer. Do you have a pocket knife?"

He shook his head, so Lauren went to the kitchen to find something to cut the tape with.

"Whatcha doing?" Nick leaned against the wall, watching her search through the drawer.

She held up a knife with a grin.

He put up his hands. "Whoa now. It looks like you're going to open those boxes. Are you sure you want to do that?"

Before she could respond, her phone buzzed in her robe pocket. She retrieved it and found three messages from William.

"Apparently, my stepbrother has decided he's

going to move in. He says he'll be here in a few days and he'll have some items delivered. Please have them taken to his bedroom."

They both returned to the boxes in the living room.

Nick scratched the back of his neck. "You want help carrying them upstairs?"

He bent down to reach for one and she put her hand on his arm. "No. He can carry them up himself. We aren't his servants."

Nick stood. He was now in her space and her hand was still on his arm. She willed it to move, but it didn't. Nick was all man standing in front of her, and in the full daylight streaming through the window, she could see every muscle and plane of his body. Damn him for not wearing a shirt. She couldn't look away.

"Why are you rubbing my arm?" Nick's voice was husky.

She tore her gaze from his chest and was startled by the heat in his eyes. Her hands went to her face as she backed away. "I'm sorry. I'm..." She was at a loss for words. Who the hell does that?

"Horny?"

Her hands fell to her sides. "Excuse me?"

He wore that crooked grin again. "You trailed off. I was just finishing your sentence for you."

She balled her fists at her sides. "Look, I'll admit from the neck down, you're an attractive man."

"The neck down? What the fu—"

"And I'll admit it's been a while since I've been with a man, so your simply being male is enough to get me going."

Nick crossed his arms, the grin gone.

"But nothing is going to happen between us, because, frankly, I don't like you."

A muscle in his jaw twitched as he eyed her. "You really know how to flatter a man. It's becoming clear why it's been a while."

What the hell? She was just being honest. She matched his stance and crossed her arms. "Well, if you can't take the truth, then you can leave."

With that, he moved forward and was in her space again, so she instantly backed away and hit the wall. Putting one hand on each side of her, he boxed her in. Then he leaned down and stared long and hard at her, causing desire to pool between her legs. He was calling her on her bullshit, and there was no denying the chemistry between them at that moment.

He reached for the tie on her robe. Slowly. Giving her time to stop him. She didn't. With one quick jerk, the robe fell open. He shifted closer until they were nearly touching.

Her skimpy nightgown now seemed to provide too much coverage.

His lips grazed her neck, then her earlobe. If it weren't for the wall, she'd fall into a puddle before him.

"Lauren." His hot breath slid over her skin. He pulled back, gazing into her eyes. She could get lost in those mocha irises.

"You can lie to yourself all you want, but don't for a second lie to me. We both know you're attracted to me. But you were right about one thing."

"What?" She couldn't believe how husky her voice was.

"Nothing can happen between us." He moved away from her, and she shivered from the absence of his body. Then he spun on his heel and went into the kitchen, leaving her there almost panting and still smelling his musky scent.

"You're a jackass!" she called after him.

"You better watch out. Showering me with all that flattery might just go to my head."

She stayed against the wall, trying to compose herself. Damn it. He was right. As much as she fought it, she was attracted to him.

A knock at the door pulled her from her lust-induced thoughts. She glanced toward the kitchen. Nick was pouring something. Then she heard the telltale sound of the top of the coffee pot clicking. He was making coffee. Most likely, he hadn't heard the knock.

She peered out the peephole and groaned. Why the hell was he here so early?

When she yanked open the door, Scott smiled and held out a ridiculously large bouquet.

"Hey, honey. I hope I didn't wake you."

Lauren inhaled slowly to calm herself. What was it with men today?

"I'm not your honey. Why are you here?"

Scott continued to hold out the flowers, but Lauren crossed her arms to let him know he wasn't buying back her love. If he thought a few gifts would erase the memory of him fucking his assistant, he had another thing coming.

"Look, Lauren, I made a mistake. I'm so sorry. You know I was under so much stress from my dad."

Her head fell back, and she shook it. Then after taking a deep breath, she looked into his eyes. "You were also so stressed out from your dad that you couldn't have sex with me. At least, that was why you told me you weren't interested all those months. But somehow, that same stress allowed you to fall dick-first into your assistant? Is that what you're saying, Scott?"

His mouth fell open. Yep, the ass had the nerve to forget he'd used the same excuse for why he didn't want sex.

"How long?"

He frowned. "What?"

"How long were you fucking your assistant?" She was practically yelling.

"It doesn't matter."

"Yes, it does. I already heard it from her, but now I need to hear it from you."

He took a step back. "She told you?"

She crossed her arms and arched a brow. If she said anything else, he'd know she was lying.

"Shit, Lauren. A few months mainly."

"Mainly?"

"After you lost your mom, you pulled away from me, from us. I tried to be there for you, but I got lonely. I made a mistake."

Then Scott's eyes nearly bugged out of his head as he looked behind Lauren.

"Who's that?"

Lauren turned to see Nick slowly walking out of the kitchen, his gaze moving from her to her ex-boyfriend standing in the doorway.

Nick was still shirtless and wearing those jeans that hung so low on his hips. He looked like a wet dream.

She turned back to her ex, ready to explain why a detective was shirtless in her house when an idea hit her.

Before she could think it through, she blurted, "This is Nick. My boyfriend. Nick, this is Scott, my ex."

Scott's jaw fell open as his gaze went from Nick's bare chest to her robe.

"Boyfriend? We just broke up. When did you find the time for this?" He waved his hand at Nick.

Nick caught on and was right there, snaking his arm around her waist. "It's new."

"New?" Scott looked like he'd sucked on a lemon. "And you're already sleeping with him?"

"You have some nerve—" Lauren began to say.

"Hell yeah." Nick spun her in his arms. "You can't fight this kind of chemistry. Isn't that right, *babe*?"

Oh no, he was going to kiss her. She had to go with it. Maybe this would get her ex to leave her alone.

Nick slowly leaned in, giving her a chance to stop him. A smirk twitched at his lips. Then he touched his forehead to hers and smiled. "Yep. I got lucky finding Lauren."

That was it? No kiss? A snuggle wasn't enough to give Scott the message she'd moved on. The challenge in Nick's eyes told her she'd have to cave first. She smirked back. She'd show him. "That's right, *babe*, you did."

Before he could pull away, her hand was behind his neck, pulling him down until their lips crashed together.

Chapter Nine

The moment he walked into the room and saw some man with Lauren, he went red with jealously. That stopped him in his tracks. He wasn't the jealous type. Plus, Lauren wasn't his girl. But something about the way the guy was hovering over her didn't sit right with him. He walked up slowly, trying to listen. The guy was holding a large bouquet of flowers. He had to be her douchebag ex.

Then when Lauren's eyes found him, they almost pleaded. After she said Nick was her boyfriend, he knew he'd play along.

At that point, he also knew he was going to push her. But maintaining his self-control was nearly impossible. He put his hands on her, expecting her to pull away. She didn't, and he liked how she felt.

But then he leaned down and touched his

forehead to hers, and she shocked him when she tugged him down and devoured him right there in her entryway. Well, damn. Maybe he didn't know Lauren as well as he thought he did.

Their tongues tangled, and suddenly, he couldn't get enough of her. She kissed as hard as she fought him. His hands slid down to her ass and cupped it. That was when the sound of someone coughing broke the spell.

He stepped away from her, and she was staring at him with the same look of hunger that he felt.

Damn, what was he doing? He was supposed to remain professional. He'd been doing a piss poor job of that. Just being around her clouded his judgment.

Scott glowered at them as he told Lauren, "Clearly, you're only doing this for revenge. I'll let you have your fling, but know this, Lauren—we were meant to be together. You'll find your way back to me soon enough. Hopefully before you soil your reputation in this town."

"Soil her reputation? Who says that?" Nick asked, trying to figure out what Lauren had seen in this guy.

The man stood tall, hands on his hips as he addressed Nick. "This is a small town. If Lauren intends to live here, it's best she not let it get around she's cheating on me."

Chasing Her Trust

"I'm not cheating on you!" Lauren yelled as she pulled away from Nick. "You cheated on me!"

Nick watched, fascinated. Lauren was getting wound up, and he thought she might deck the guy. On one hand, he was an officer who should try to stop that, but on the other, this guy really needed to get decked.

When she shifted closer to her ex, his hands went to her shoulders and Nick tensed. That man's hands did not belong on her.

"Honey, we've been together a long time. It makes sense we needed a break. One last hurrah, if you will. Take a couple of days and then we'll talk."

Scott patted her on the shoulder, which looked more like a dad move than a boyfriend one. This guy had no game. But fortunately, he turned and was about to leave.

Before Nick could even get his sigh of relief out, Lauren yelled after Scott, "He's not a fling. We're living together!"

Shit.

Scott spun around, and if it were possible for steam to come out of his ears, it would have. His neck and face flushed read and he glared at Nick.

"You're serious?" Scott asked.

"I am." Lauren looped her arm through Nick's and smiled up at him.

"How did you two meet anyway?" Scott crossed his arms, staring at both of them skeptically.

Lauren froze. Nick figured honesty was the best way to go.

"At the grocery store in town. I was picking up dinner and she bought a large pack of water bottles. I helped her get it in the trunk and it was just love at first sight. Isn't that right, *pumpkin*?" he said with extra emphasis on the endearment.

She flashed him a smile. "That's right, boo."

He suppressed a chuckle at her attempt at an endearment for him.

"I don't believe we formally met." Scott walked back up to the porch and extended his hand. "Scott Fisher."

Nick pulled his arm free from Lauren and shook it. "Detective Nick Moore."

Scott nodded. "You're the guy who took Joey's job? I've heard about you."

"I didn't take anyone's job."

"Well, I suspect I'll be seeing a lot more of you, Detective Nick Moore."

Scott turned and walked to his car with a waddle that confirmed Nick's suspicion that he likely had a stick up his ass.

Nick and Lauren remained in the doorway until Scott had driven out of sight. Then Nick took a step back from her. "Mind telling me what the hell just happened?"

"I'm sorry. He wouldn't leave me alone and I figured if he thought you were my boyfriend, he would."

"Is that really the reason?" Nick grinned.

Her brow furrowed. "What other reason would there be?"

He moved into her space again, could feel the heat radiating off her body. "I've seen the way you look at me. You could have been upfront and told me you want me. There's no need to ask me to be your pretend boyfriend."

She leaned away from him. "What? No! How arrogant are you?"

He laughed. "You're easy to rile. Too fun."

She stormed past him to the living room. He followed.

"I'm sorry. I just meant—"

Before he could finish his sentence, she was beating him with a throw pillow she'd somehow grabbed.

"Wait!" He held up his hands to defend himself.

But she kept going, a look of strong determination on her face that he found cute and hilarious at the same time.

In one quick move, he grabbed the pillow, tossing it on the couch while pulling her back to his chest with his right arm. Then he used his left one to pin her to his body.

"You feel better?"

She nodded.

God, she felt good against him. But he needed to keep it professional. "Good. How are we going to say we broke up?"

She spun in his arms. "We can't break up!"

Her body was flush against his. Well, this made it very hard to stay professional. Thank God he was wearing jeans, because his *interest* was quickly growing, and that was the last thing he wanted her to feel right now.

"What do you mean we can't break up?" When the hoarseness in his voice surprised them both, he released her, and she moved away.

"If we break up, Scott will pursue me again. You heard him—he thinks this is some fling and I'll eventually go back to him."

"I can't pretend to date you."

She rolled her eyes. "Worried I'm going to cockblock you? Is that it?"

Was that a hint of jealousy he caught in her voice? Fuck, no. It didn't matter. He shook his head. *Focus.*

"No, I'm worried I'll lose my job. Chief Dunin made it clear I had to watch out for the Chanler family, give them special attention."

She grinned. "Well, you can let Dunin know you're giving me special attention." She winked. She actually winked at him, and damn if that didn't turn him on more.

"No, I don't think he'd appreciate that."

"I'm sorry, Nick, but I think he's going to find out."

"No, he won't. Because we just broke up." He stormed up the stairs. He needed a shower, a cold one. This woman was driving him crazy.

He went to his room and sat on his bed. How the hell would he explain this to the chief if he found out? The only solution was that the chief could never hear about this. He only needed to last six months here, then he could move on.

"Nick." Lauren was in his doorway. "Scott announced our relationship on social media a few minutes ago." She held up her phone.

He jumped up and grabbed it, growling as he read the post. "Just found out Detective Nick Moore stole my girl. I'm in shreds over this."

"Guess we're official," Lauren said.

Shit.

After Nick set her phone on the nightstand, he fell back on his bed and rubbed his eyes. Then he sat up. "Wait, the chief probably won't even see it. I don't do social media, because of my job. He probably doesn't either."

Lauren cocked her head. "Nick, this is a small town. Someone will tell him. Besides, Harvey's already commented on it. Apparently, he does social media and he doesn't like you. I'm guessing he'll fill in the chief."

Nick picked the phone back up and clicked to

read the comments. Sure enough, Harvey was right up top. "Knew I didn't like that guy," he grumbled, and fell back onto the bed again with a groan.

"If Dunin gives you any grief, let me know. My aunt seems to know him well."

Fuck. All he had to do was stay at this job, do well, and then he could reapply for a position with his old department. How hard could that be? But this, this could ruin his entire career. He had to be careful.

"Damn it, Lauren. We'll have to tell the chief this is fake."

"We can't!"

"I could lose my job." He rubbed his temples.

"You're not going to lose your job if we are truly in love. Just tell Dunin that."

He sat up. "Truly in love after a few days?"

"Hey, you told Scott it was love at first sight. Let's go with that."

Her robe had fallen open a bit at the top and there was a small patch of pink lace peeking out. She followed his gaze to it, then cinched the robe shut.

"Well, if we're deeply in love, perhaps there are a few other perks we could explore." He waggled his eyebrows.

"I'm sorry, Nick, but I'm waiting for marriage."

His jaw dropped. "You're not going to tell anyone that are you? No one would believe I'd be that patient."

"Oh? You can't go without sex? I figured at

your age that wouldn't be a problem."

"What?"

She ignored his question. "If we're in love, we should probably know a few things about each other. How old are you?"

"Thirty-one. And not old enough to go without."

"We'll see. You know, if we're together, you can't be with anyone else."

"Not a problem, but I'm not telling people we're waiting. That would make it harder to explain when you succumb to my charms."

She laughed. "That won't happen. Have you ever been married? Any kids?"

"No and no. You?"

Her smile fell. "No, I had been with Scott for a long time. Thought I'd marry him someday."

Why would the feisty, gorgeous woman in front of him fall for a douche like that?

"What did you see in him?"

She walked over and sat next to Nick on the bed. His fingers itched to pull her closer, but he controlled himself.

"When I first met him, he was home on break his senior year in college. The whole town was excited for him, they practically threw him a parade. Evidently, he was good at football. Anyway, we met, and despite all of this attention everyone was giving him, *his* attention was solely on me."

That's all it took? is what Nick wanted to say, but instead, he asked her, "And you fell for that?"

She shoved him away. "Can you try to be less judgmental?"

He shrugged.

"No, I liked it, but then we both went away to finish our senior years and I didn't see him again until the summer after we both graduated. I'd come back to work at the diner. It was what I did when I was here for the summer. He came in, asked me out, and that was it."

"Please tell me he took you out on some nice dates or something. How long before the douche side came out?"

Lauren's phone buzzed from the nightstand.

She ignored it and continued to explain. "It came out slowly. Honestly, I never realized until I walked in on him having sex with his assistant."

Controlling the anger in his voice, Nick asked, "He cheated on you?"

She nodded. "He claims it was just her and it didn't last long."

"But you don't believe him?"

Her phone buzzed again.

"No."

"Someone's trying to reach you." Nick grabbed her phone and handed it to her. She sat down on the bed next to him, then groaned when she looked at the screen.

"What's wrong?" he asked.

"Looks like you went from most hated Detective to most hated man in this town." She turned her phone so he could see the posts.

The first one read "First he takes Joey's job. Now he's taking Scott's girl. Who the hell does this guy think he is?"

The next several posts weren't any better.

She licked her lips. "Maybe it's not as bad as you think."

He quirked a brow.

"All right, so maybe it is. But we didn't do anything wrong. *You* didn't do anything wrong. Go out there and hold your head high." She nodded for emphasis.

"You want to go out there with me? Arm in arm?"

Her eyes widened. "Um, actually, I'm supposed to be at work soon."

"Me too."

"Let's meet back here tonight and come up with a plan."

"Sounds good," Nick said.

She didn't move and neither did he. He didn't want to. She was staring at his lips.

"Lauren?"

She blinked and looked up at him. "What?"

"What were you thinking just now?"

Her eyes darted to his mouth and then to the

door as her cheeks flushed red. "I need to go."

She was thinking about their kiss. He was sure of it because he was doing the same thing.

Chapter Ten

Shit. Shit. Shit.

If one more person glared at her, she was going to scream. She wasn't the bad guy here! Plastering on a happy face, Lauren walked into the diner. As she headed toward her locker, she tried not to pay attention to a few women bending their heads down and whispering. She was almost to the back when she stopped in her tracks at what she overheard.

"Who in their right mind would give up a man like Scott Fisher? He's the town catch, for goodness sake."

Spinning on her heel, she stomped over to the table. Normally, she would've had more restraint — or more manners, as her mom liked to call them. But not today and not when it came to Scott.

"Scott is not the catch you all think he is."

"Lauren! I need to see you now," was called out from the back.

Great! Her boss caught her chewing out the customers.

Moving to the kitchen, she came toe to toe with Logan.

"Lauren, there's been a lot of talk about you in here this morning. I know everyone's acting like Scott is some god we need to all bow down to." Logan shook his head. "I went to school with him. I know him. You were too good for him. I'm sorry you're going through this."

"Thank you," she told him, surprised. At least there was one person in this town she could count on to have her back. Plus, Harmony. And, strangely, now Nick.

"Anyway, if anyone gives you too much crap, let me know. I'll take care of them."

Lauren thanked him, and as she was putting on her apron, Logan patted her on the shoulder and went into his office. Then she steeled herself to go to the front and face those women. But before she got through the doorway, Harmony came in the rear entrance.

"Oh my God! Tell me it's true. Please let it be true!"

"Is what true?"

Harmony jumped up and down. "Are you

dating Detective McHottie? Please say yes and tell me all about it. Damn, that man is fine."

Lauren shook her head. "Wait, I thought you didn't like him because he took Joey's job."

Her friend waved her hand. "First, we all know Joey didn't step away for family purposes or whatever bullshit the chief is selling. Second, I don't need to like him to want to bone him. Or live vicariously through you boning him." She waggled her eyebrows.

"Ugh! No one's boning anyone."

Harmony crossed her arms. "I can see that. You're way too grumpy to be getting boned. So then what's this that Scott's posting?"

Lauren quickly filled her friend in on the morning's activities. "And now I have a room full of women that think *I'm* the cheater. Can you believe it?"

Harmony snorted. "Yeah. I wish I'd known you before you met Scott. I would have told you not to go out with that man."

"You already told me he was a dick in high school, but even you thought he'd changed!"

Harmony grimaced. "I did say that, didn't I? Sorry. He's still an asshole."

"Can you just help me get through this shift without killing anyone?"

Her friend saluted her. "Yes, sir. I can do that." She turned and Lauren followed her out to a full lunch crowd.

The rest of the day went fast. Only a few hiccups where Harmony took over a table or two. Bless her soul, Harmony even told a few people off. And Logan threatened one woman with a permanent ban. All in all, it was a most eventful day at Lucky's Diner.

At the end of Lauren's shift, there was only one table of lingerers left to close out the bill for and then she could go home and take a long, hot shower.

As she approached with their check, the woman with her back to Lauren didn't hear her coming.

"That man still has a room over at the motel. If he was really serious about her and living with her, why would he still have his motel room?" All eyes at the table were wide as Lauren's hands went to her hips.

"He's stepping out on her. Serves her right for what she did to Scott."

"Tabitha." Her friend jerked her head in Lauren's direction. The woman turned and her hand went to her mouth.

"Oh, I'm sorry, I didn't—"

"Know I was standing behind you? Clearly. For the record, I was with Scott for six long years. I never cheated on him. You know what ended our relationship? The fact he'd been fucking his assistant. Yeah, walking in on that was a shocker. But look at it this way, he can be all yours." She dropped the bill on the table and marched to the back.

"Are you all right?" Harmony's hands were on her shoulders.

"Yeah, I'm okay.

"What did they say?"

"Doesn't matter." Lauren went to her locker and grabbed her purse. "I need to go. Can you get their payment?"

"Of course."

Lauren went out the back door to her car. Once inside, she let the tears fall. "Damn it, Scott. You just keep ruining my life."

★ ★ ★

Never had Nick felt such relief leaving a police station. The entire day had been a shit show thanks to Scott and his post.

The moment he walked in this morning, the chief was growling. After getting his ass chewed, he tried to explain his relationship with Lauren was a sudden thing he couldn't deny. God, he sounded like an ass. He wanted to be truthful with Dunin, but he knew Dunin would tell Scott's dad. Dunin had made it clear several times in their conversation that he and Mr. Fisher went way back. Scott was like a son to him.

Nick didn't hesitate to explain that Scott had

been the one to cheat and was turning it around in some jealous tantrum. Dunin nodded.

"Scott is used to getting what he wants. If he thinks he can win Lauren back, he'll stoop low to get there. Watch yourself."

Nick kept his mouth closed after that, despite having a lot he wanted to say.

Finally, Dunin saw reason—that Nick's personal life was none of his business. That left Nick free to make progress on the pile of work on his desk. Apparently, Joey had been spending all his time out in the field and never completed any paperwork. Following up on someone else's cases and working long after the fact was damn near impossible, but if that meant everyone would leave him alone, he'd take it.

The entire day passed with no calls for his services. He couldn't help but believe that was more than a coincidence. Especially when Harvey came rolling in just before five and flopped into his desk chair. "Been extra busy for me today. Looks like no one wants to work with you." Harvey scowled at him.

Fuck. He had to work with this man. Might as well clear the air. "I didn't steal her away. What Scott said was bullshit."

"Oh yeah? You have a history of stealing things that aren't yours."

"I didn't steal this job either!"

"That's enough!" Dunin stood in his office

doorway, glaring at them. "Moore's right. He didn't steal Joey's job. Joey wasn't fit to do it anymore. You know that as well as I do, Harvey. Now, both of you, go home, but keep your phones on."

Dunin went back into his office and slammed the door.

Nick grabbed his coat from his chair and walked out before Harvey could say another word. He'd promised Lauren this morning he'd stay at the mansion again. She was worried whoever ransacked the place might return. He was glad she'd asked, because his gut told him he should be there, although he wasn't sure how much that had to do with the case versus that kiss they'd shared in front of Scott.

Damn that kiss. She'd taken him by surprise with that. Now he couldn't' think about anything else.

Before he put himself back in her orbit, he needed time to cool off from the day he'd had. When he strolled past the diner on the way to Zach's pub, he saw Lauren inside talking to a few women. He stopped and stared. She was stunning, even in her ridiculous pink uniform shirt. Living under the same roof with her was going to be challenging. Especially if he heard any buzzing coming from her room again. He chuckled, remembering how embarrassed she'd gotten about that.

It was a short walk, and as he took everything in, he tried to focus on the decorated storefronts, the people, the town itself—anything but Lauren.

This town was certainly more cheerful than where he used to live, and he could probably grow to like it here if it weren't for everyone being so small-minded. Damn, had he been this small-minded in his old town?

Not that it mattered. He needed to stick to his plan and get out of here in six months. Then he could get his career back on track. He would have to prove himself to his old boss, Dwight, but he was confident he could do it.

Nick reached the pub, which had a sign in the window that read "Brannigan's." When he stepped inside, the place was about what he'd expected, with a large bar, several big screen TVs, and a few dartboards scattered on the walls.

"Hey, Nick! Glad you could make it in," Zach shouted from behind the bar as if they were old friends.

Nick nodded and took a seat on a barstool.

"What can I get for you?"

"I'll take an IPA if you have it."

Zach nodded and grabbed a glass and started filling it.

"I guess you didn't heed that warning I gave you," Zach said as he placed the beer in front of Nick.

Nick chuckled. "Guess not."

"You're quite the topic around here. You're stealing things left and right, they say."

Nick took a gulp of the beer.

"First a job, then the golden boy's girl. You've become the town pariah."

Nick shrugged. "I'm the new guy. It was bound to happen."

Zach leaned on the counter. "Is it true? Are you really dating Lauren?"

"It's a long story."

Zach spread his arms. "I got time."

"Do you know William Chanler?"

The bartender whistled. "He's a piece of work. Have you met him?"

Nick shook his head.

"Well, if you do, expect him to treat you like the hired help. Seriously, he'll ask you to carry his bags or bring his tea or some such shit."

Well, that made sense with how William had handled the delivery of his boxes.

"When the whole town was at Michael Chanler's funeral, William wasn't behaving right."

"What do you mean?"

"In the middle of the service, William's phone rang."

"So, he forgot to turn it off," Nick reasoned, then took another drink of his beer.

"He stepped out to the lobby and took the call."

"Maybe it was a relative."

"No. It wasn't. I followed him out, and he was talking to someone about paying them later. It was a business call." He wiped down the bar as he spoke.

"You followed him?"

Zach shrugged. "I was curious."

Nick arched a brow.

"All right, I don't like funerals. I needed air and figured I'd see what William was up to. Anyway, it was his dad's funeral. It's not right that he was taking business calls."

"What does William do for business?"

"He's the CEO of Chanler Enterprises. He works out of their Portland office."

"Portland? But his dad lived here?"

"Two offices. Hey, if the rumor's true, and you're living at the mansion, you'll meet him soon enough. I heard he's coming to town."

"Where did you hear that?"

"Scott's dad was in here earlier and mentioned it. Odd, though, since William only visits in July. But I'm sure he has matters to take care of now that his dad is gone."

"Hey, stranger. You're new in town." Nick heard the female voice and when he glanced over, a tall, thin brunette stood next to him.

"Buy me a drink?" she asked.

Zach frowned at Nick. He knew what Zach was thinking and he was happy to prove him wrong.

"Sorry. I don't think my girlfriend would much care for that. Thanks for the beer, Zach. I have to go."

Chasing Her Trust

He swiveled off the stool and walked to the door. When he reached for his phone, he realized he'd left it on the bar. Hopefully, it was still there. When he circled back, he saw Scott Fisher talking to the woman who'd just hit on him.

The man had tried to set him up. The chief was right. Scott would stoop low.

Chapter Eleven

As Lauren headed home, she didn't know whether to hunt Scott down for his post or to come clean to everyone. The whole town now thought she'd cheated on him and that he was the victim. The worst part was that everyone so easily believed it. She might not have grown up here, but she thought she'd made friends since she'd been working at the diner. Apparently, no one ever considered that Scott, Mr. Captain of the Football Team, would ever cheat. Ugh. When she told off that one group at the diner, she didn't think for a minute they actually believed her.

She drove right up to the front of the mansion. The garage sat mostly empty, but she never felt right parking in there. It used to house several of her stepdad's collector cars, but those went to his son, William, after he died.

She stomped up the porch stairs and inside, slamming the door behind her. But her body was wound tight with tension that no amount of slamming doors would relieve.

Then the memory of kissing Nick in that exact spot flooded her. Damn he'd felt so good. If Scott hadn't been standing right there, she might have kept going.

Of course, if it weren't for Scott, she and Nick wouldn't have kissed in the first place. They didn't even like each other. Nick had only played a game of chicken and lost spectacularly. Spectacular. That was a great way to describe that kiss. One she hoped to repeat soon.

No. What was she thinking? This was Nick. The man who'd brushed off her valid complaint that first night he came here. He wasn't someone she should be having sexy thoughts about.

She'd simply gone too long without any sex. That's all this was. And a lack of sex she could fix — well, sort of.

Marching up the stairs to her room, she locked the door and reached into her nightstand for her vibrator. Nick had texted earlier to say he'd be late. Since he didn't have a key, she told him she'd leave one under the mat, which she hadn't done yet. But before she got to that, she had to relieve the ache between her legs that had been there since this morning. There was no way he'd overhear her this time.

She shrugged off her coat and was about to undress when someone knocked on her bedroom door.

Fear swelled up in her. Nick couldn't have gotten in. Or could he? Did she lock the door? She couldn't remember. It was probably Grace.

Another knock. "Lauren, it's William."

She sighed with relief that it wasn't an intruder. Not that she was thrilled to see William. It was odd that he was staying here this time of the year.

When she opened the door, his large frame was leaning against the wall. He was nearly twenty years older than her but looked even older than the last time she saw him. He was a known workaholic and it showed. He spent all his time at his desk or in meetings and did nothing to take care of himself.

"I just wanted to let you know I'll be staying here for a while. I didn't want you to get scared if you heard a noise in my room," he told her, then his eyes raked over her body and she crossed her arms to head off where they were going. He'd never looked at her like that and she had no idea why he was now.

"I heard you and Scott broke up."

Ah. That was why.

"Yep." She needed to change the subject fast. That's when she noticed he had black circles under his eyes. He either hadn't been sleeping or... "Were you in a fight?" That didn't make sense. William was the last person she could imagine fighting anyone.

"No. No. I'm just tired. I haven't been sleeping well."

His gaze moved to the bed and his brows shot up. Lauren turned and saw her bright pink vibrator sitting in the middle of it. Shit. No denying what that was.

"You know, Lauren, if you need some help with that, I'm available. I've been told I'm pretty good."

A little bit of vomit came up at his suggestion. While he wasn't technically her brother, they'd been part of the same family for a long time.

William stood there so confident. Apparently, being rich and the CEO of Chanler Enterprises had allowed him to get any woman he wanted. At least that was what his confidence suggested.

"No. That won't be necessary."

William crossed his arms. "I'm not usually turned down when it comes to a quick hook up."

Lauren frowned. William saying "hook up" sounded like an adult trying to fit in with the kids. It wasn't right.

"Uh, sorry. Not tonight."

William's smile returned. "Then us hooking up another time is still on the table?"

"What? No! That's gross! We're family."

He shoved his hands in his pockets. "Well, actually, we aren't. At least, not anymore."

"Go away, William. And never bring this up again."

She shut and locked her door and listened for him to walk away. All she heard was silence. After a several minutes, there was a quiet chuckle and then his footsteps faded toward his room.

William had always given her the creeps, but he'd never actually hit on her before. Thank God Nick was staying at the house. Hopefully, Grace would be there a while too. Anything to avoid being alone with William.

All she probably had to do was tell him Nick was her boyfriend. Now they were going to have to also pretend inside the house, not only in public. God, did that mean they had to share a room? She shook that thought away. No, they'd figure it out.

Why was William here anyway? He never visited during the holidays. Something Lauren had always thought was odd. He had an excuse every time—some deal was about to close or some other work-related emergency. Then he would send her, her mom, and his dad expensive gifts.

Of course, maybe his family had never been big on spending the holidays together. Once her mom and Robert married, they took long cruises during the holidays. Her mom explained that since Lauren was in college and didn't come home much outside of summer break, they just weren't going to do the traditional Christmas anymore.

She could still taste the disappointment. Christmas had always been one of her favorite times of year. When it was only her and her mom, Lauren had made it home every year to spend it with her. They would decorate a tree and have hot chocolate. It was their tradition.

Using her sleeve, she wiped her eyes, and the bright pink vibrator caught her attention. After the run-in with her stepbrother, she definitely wasn't in the mood anymore. Besides, what if he heard her? Oh God. That was a visual that would do her in for months, if not years. She put it away and sat on her bed. Her stomach growled. She was hungry but really didn't want to chance facing him again. Then the front door opened and closed. Butterflies danced in her stomach.

For a second, she thought maybe it was Nick. Then she remembered she still had the damn key. She cursed herself. She shouldn't be this excited to see her fake boyfriend, the man she couldn't stand.

No, this was more about having someone there as a buffer for William. That's all this was.

Lauren went downstairs and heard something in the kitchen. As she approached, she realized it was someone humming.

Grace.

When she walked in, her aunt was turning on the oven. On the counter was a bag that Lauren hoped was full of food.

"Hi," Lauren said.

Grace spun around and smiled. "Good evening." Her aunt's smile could light up a room.

"You're in a good mood. Are the renovations going well?"

Grace looked confused. "Renovations?"

"On your house."

Her eyes lit up. "Oh! Yes, they are. And now I'm going to cook us up something to celebrate. But first, we should do happy hour."

"Happy hour?"

Grace went to an area of the kitchen that was set up like a bar. Lauren's stepdad threw a few parties each summer, and this was where he always made a signature cocktail and then served it in a punch bowl.

Lauren sat at the table and watched as Grace started mixing. The sound of crystal clinking must have drifted upstairs, because soon, William appeared in the doorway.

"William! You're home!" Grace walked over and pulled him in for a big hug. "I've missed you. You stay away too much."

He hugged her back. "I'm sorry. I just get so busy, you know."

"Well, I'm glad you're here. I'm making something special for happy hour. You want some?"

"You know I do. You make the best drinks. Here, I bought this in case you want any."

Grace took the bottle from William and

examined it. "Whistle Pig. Wow. You have good taste." She set it down on the bar, then told him, "Sit down. I'll bring the drinks over when I'm finished."

William turned his attention to Lauren. "Lauren, you look more relaxed. What have you been up to?" He smirked.

She squeezed her lids shut and willed the embarrassment to go away to no avail. "Nope, still quite tense," she clarified.

"Here we are." Grace set two drinks on the table, then returned to the counter for hers.

The drink was brown and smelled like ginger. Lauren took a small sip and struggled to swallow it. When her eyes met Grace's, she smiled. Grace was a fantastic cook and took pride in everything she made. There was no way Lauren was going to break her heart and tell her the drink was bad.

"Take another sip, dear. Trust me," Grace said.

"This is fantastic, Grace. You always make the best drinks," William said. "I'll be right back. I forgot I need to make a call."

"Thank you, William."

Grace pulled a container out of her bag, took the lid off, and slid it into the oven. Then she prepared a green salad.

Lauren tasted her drink again, and Grace was right, a sweet flavor hit her tongue this time. As she continued to sip, her mind wandered to Nick. She had no idea what time he would be done with work. He might get in after she went to bed. The thought disappointed her.

"That'll be ready in about thirty minutes." Grace set the timer on the oven.

William entered the room again, holding his empty glass. "You added bitters. Love it." He went straight to the bar and filled it to the rim with something brown.

He caught Lauren watching him and laughed. "I've got a long evening of work ahead of me. Figure I need the fortitude." He nodded to her and then said, "Grace, thank you again. I'll be up in my room working the rest of the night."

"But, William, you must have dinner with us. It's a large lasagna. Plenty for all of us."

He gave Grace a smile. "Sure. I probably should eat. I'll come back down later."

After William left, Grace took a seat next to Lauren. "Do you have some news to tell me, dear?"

"News?"

Grace arched a brow.

Lauren groaned. "You heard." Her head met the table. She did not want to discuss Scott anymore today.

"The rumor is you cheated on Scott and he's heartbroken." Grace leaned back in her chair. "What really happened?"

Lauren sat up. "You don't believe the rumor?"

Grace laughed. "You forget. I know that boy."

"Scott cheated and now he's trying to make me look like the bad guy," Lauren confided in her.

"He just wants to save face. This is his hometown."

"Yes, but he's hurting Nick. Nick could lose his job over this."

Grace smiled. "So it's true. You are dating the new detective. Is he as hot as the rumors say he is?"

Lauren's body warmed, remembering their kiss. Hot didn't even begin to describe it.

"Based on your flush, he must be."

With the way she was feeling, Lauren knew she was in trouble when it came to Nick.

Chapter Twelve

Nick couldn't believe how close he'd come to telling Zach the relationship was fake. No wonder Zach's pub was so successful. In no time flat, he'd had Nick feeling so comfortable, he was ready to spill his feelings and secrets. Nick wasn't one to share anything. That was an important skill in his line of work. Thankfully, he'd come to his senses. It also helped that Zach had left him alone the moment the leggy brunette sat next to him.

He hadn't been that blatantly hit on in years. He should have known it was a set up. Hell, no one in this town was happy he and Lauren were supposedly together.

Lauren. She was all he could think about on the drive home. That and sleep. One bad night in the car and he'd been paying for it for days. But when he pulled the mat back, there was no key. He yanked his phone out of his pocket and called Lauren.

"Nick?"

"There's no key," he huffed out.

"Good evening to you too."

He sighed into the phone. "I'm sorry. I'm tired and I just want to go to bed."

The door flew open and his gaze went straight to Lauren's legs. She had on short, lacy shorts and some sort of pajama tank top, also lacy. Under the bright entryway light, he could see through it to her rosy nipples.

She crossed her arms, forcing him to look up into her glaring eyes. She stood in the same spot where they'd kissed that morning. He wanted to kiss her again. But he knew that wasn't a good idea.

"Good evening, babe. You wear that special for me? I thought we agreed you'd wear something less revealing." He laid on the sugary tone as he walked past her, purposely brushing up against her. Just that little touch and he was already on fire. Yeah, he needed to get to bed before he did something he would regret.

"No. But thanks for asking about my day, *babe*. It was great. Most of the town hates me for what they think I did to Scott, and they made sure to tell me. That really helps with the tips, by the way. And no, I didn't wear anything special for you."

She stormed past him, bumping into him, and

when he got his balance, he followed her into the kitchen. "Liar."

She whipped around and must not have expected him to be so close, because she immediately took a step back. When it looked like she was going to fall, he reached out and grabbed her waist, pulling her to him. The damn lace was so thin that she might as well have been naked as she was pressed up against him.

"What are you doing?" Her hands were on his chest, pushing him away.

As all his blood continued to rush south, he could barely think. Finally, he forced out the words, "Stopping you from falling. You almost toppled over." He removed his hands and she swayed a bit.

"Have you been drinking?"

Now her hands were on her hips and she shifted forward and got in his face. God, the lights were also bright in here, so he could still see her nipples. Wait. Either she was cold, or she was feeling this just as much as he was.

"Yes, but I wasn't about to fall over. And I don't need you making some lame ass excuse to get your hands on me."

His hands shot up in the air. "I'm not trying to get my hands on you—"

"And what I wanted to tell you before your stunt—"

"Stunt? I don't think—"

"Was that while I may have said you were my boyfriend, you were the one who pushed Scott over the line by putting your arms around me for a kiss," she whispered.

"Me?!" he boomed. No, she did not get to change what really happened. "Pumpkin"—he made sure to pop the second *p* for emphasis—"I merely put my arms around you. You were the one who kissed me. And why are you whispering?" He glanced around but didn't see anyone else.

"William's here. And he has to think we're the real deal, by the way. As for the kiss… You know."

He grinned. This just got interesting. "Why does William have to believe that? And regarding the kiss—no, actually, I don't know. Enlighten me."

She sucked her bottom lip into her teeth. "You kissed me like you wanted me." She spoke quietly.

"I'm sorry. I didn't hear you. What was that?" He couldn't stop from goading her.

"Like you wanted me. You did it on purpose, and now Scott's on the warpath."

He moved closer to her and could feel the warmth of her body. And when his gaze met hers, it took all the control he had not to lean down and capture those plump lips.

"Lauren, I think you forgot something very important."

Her eyes went to his mouth. Yeah, she wanted to be kissed.

"What's that?" She leaned forward a little, just enough.

All he had to do was move another inch, and they'd be back where they were this morning. But he still couldn't stop himself from egging her on. "You kissed me," he whispered. "And I could tell you wanted me."

The passion in her eyes transformed to anger in almost an instant. He took a step back out of self-preservation.

"My first impression was right. You're so full of yourself."

The corner of his mouth curled up, and he couldn't stop the smile. "I'm a confident guy. Nothing wrong with that."

"So confident that you think I threw myself at you? Think again, Nick. You won't be kissing me again." She stormed past him and started up the stairs.

"You got one thing right."

She stopped and turned. "What's that?"

"I won't be kissing you again. Not until you beg me for it."

Her eyes narrowed as he struggled to maintain a straight face.

"Good. I'm glad we're on the same page," she said, then ascended the stairs.

"Wait," he called after her.

She came back down. "What?"

"You didn't answer my question. Why does William need to believe we're together?"

She rolled her eyes. "He thinks I'm single now and he hit on me. He creeps me out. I'd feel more comfortable here if he thought I was with you."

"Your *stepbrother*?" he asked.

"He doesn't think of me in a sisterly way."

Nick balled his fists. "And what do you mean he hit on you? Did he touch you?"

She shook her head and her cheeks flushed as Nick crossed his arms and waited for her to explain.

"He saw my vibrator sitting on my bed and made a rude comment that he could help."

Nick closed his eyes to calm himself. First, he wanted to deck William, who he'd never even met. Then he wanted to find out why Lauren had such a need for her vibrator. It had only been two days since he'd caught her using it. What kind of sexual appetite did she have?

Nope, don't go down that road. Too late. He was already at half-mast and his pants weren't going to hide it much longer.

"I need something to drink." He took off to the kitchen, hoping she wouldn't follow him.

"Nick."

Fuck. He found a cup in the cupboard next to the sink and filled it with water. He wasn't going to ask her. But then he looked over his shoulder at her. Oh hell, he had to know.

"How often do you use your vibrator?"

He hadn't thought her face could get any redder. He'd been wrong.

"What? That's none of your business."

He spun around and in two strides had her in his arms. "Oh, I beg to differ. That's very much my business now."

"Shit, is William behind me?" she whispered.

Nick smiled, neither confirming nor denying.

"Quick, do something boyfriend-like."

He cocked his head and bit back his laugh. "What do you mean?"

She sighed. "Damn it, Nick. Kiss me!" she hissed.

He leaned down and kissed her neck, then whispered, "Are you begging?"

Her hands clutched his shirt. "Yes!"

That was all he needed. His lips crashed down on hers and it was better than their kiss that morning. He didn't hold back and neither did she. After a few minutes, she pulled away, then turned around.

"Did he go upstairs?"

"Who?" Nick's blood wasn't pumping to his brain.

"William?"

"No."

She took a step back. "Wasn't he just down here?"

"Nope. Told you you'd beg for a kiss."

"You're infuriating! I'd kick you out right now, except you know I need you."

"You're avoiding the question."

"What question?"

"How often do you use your vibrator?"

"As I told you, that's none of your business."

"It is when I can hear it through the wall."

She closed her eyes and wrapped her arms around herself.

"I'm sorry. I'm not trying to embarrass you."

"Could have fooled me! Why do you need to know?"

"Because I can hear you through the wall and I want to be the one to get you off." *Shit!* He hadn't meant to say that.

Lauren's eyes opened and welled with tears.

Double shit. He didn't expect that reaction. "What's wrong? Why is that so upsetting?"

Her hands went to her face. "Because you can't."

"I can't what?"

She flung her arms down to her sides as she shouted, "You can't get me off!"

"I'll come back for dinner later." William, who'd appeared out of nowhere, grinned as he spun on his heel and then went upstairs.

Great, now this jackass thought Nick had performance problems. He looked down at Lauren, whose tears were falling.

"God, how embarrassing." She plopped down at the kitchen table, her head hitting it when she leaned forward.

"I think it's more embarrassing for me than you. Can you tell me why you're so convinced I couldn't do the job?"

She sat up. "A man has never given me an orgasm. I've only been able to do it with my vibrator. I'm almost thirty, Nick. If it was going to happen, it would have already happened."

Anger didn't even cover what he was feeling for Scott right now. Not only did that dip shit not please his woman, but he had her convinced no man could.

He took her hands in his. "Lauren, I don't know what kind of douchebags you've dated, but I can assure you I could get you off."

She stared at him for a few seconds, then laughed.

"I wasn't trying to be funny. I'm serious."

She continued to laugh. "I know. You're so self-confident."

"No, I mean, I don't think there's anything wrong with you."

Lauren stopped laughing. "Thank you. You can be really nice sometimes. Maybe we could be friends."

Friends? Did she just friend-zone me?
"Friends?"

"Yes. Can you be my friend, Nick?"

"Sure." Because what the hell else could he say right now?

Chapter Thirteen

The next morning, Lauren stopped in her tracks when she entered the kitchen and saw William sitting at the table. Being alone with him was not her idea of a good time. Especially after yesterday. Between spotting her vibrator and hearing her admission to Nick, he knew far too much about her. But he'd seen her, and it was too late to go back upstairs.

Ignoring him for the moment, she went straight to the coffee maker and poured herself a cup. "Thanks for making coffee."

"You're welcome. I wasn't sure how much to make."

She turned back to him. "Oh, this is enough for me. Thank you."

William cocked his head. "What about your

gentleman caller?"

Gentleman caller? Who says that? Apparently older CEO types. She hadn't had a chance to mention Nick to William or Grace yet. Closing her eyes, she had to admit that wasn't true. She really didn't want to mention the ransacking. Grace would likely overreact and force them all into her small house. No, she needed space. But maybe if she told William first, he could help break the news to Grace.

"I don't have a gentleman caller," Lauren began.

"I beg to differ. He's a man and he was here for... Well, he was here. I'm sorry he wasn't able to meet your needs, though. That explains a lot."

She stared at him, too stunned to speak. Why was he bringing this up?

"Lauren, you have the right to stay here, but you don't have the right to bring your hookups back here." William maintained eye contact as he took a sip of his coffee.

What the hell?

His demeanor was cold, all business. Was this because she'd turned him down?

Setting her coffee on the counter, she clasped her hands together so she might be able to get through this without punching him in the face, then stepped forward. "First, what I do in my room is none of your business and—"

He shrugged. "It could be. The offer remains

open."

"What the actual fuck? You just said I can't have hookups here, and in the next breath, you're trying to hook up with me?"

The memory of his offer the night before made her feel sick. Her heart nearly thudded out of her chest. Why did she let William get to her so badly?

"I belong in this house. Whoever you have up there doesn't."

Through clenched teeth, she responded, "The man is a detective. He's staying in his own bedroom because the house was ransacked. We're dating, but we're not hooking up." God, she needed to stop rambling.

William's brows shot up. "Ransacked? Was anything taken?"

"Not that I could tell."

William stood so fast, the chair skidded behind him, making a loud screeching noise.

"How the hell would you know if something was missing? You don't know this place like I do. Were all the rooms ransacked?"

"Only a few downstairs," Nick said as he entered the kitchen.

Nick was again shirtless and only wore jeans and no socks. The memory of their kiss last night flooded Lauren's mind and she knew her cheeks were turning red. She was starting to regret suggesting they only be friends.

Nick winked and offered her a smile.

William crossed his arms. "Really, Lauren? There was no hookup?"

Nick frowned as he looked from William to her. "What's he talking about?"

"Detective, is it? Do you regularly walk around on the job without a shirt on?"

Nick's smile fell as he turned a serious gaze to William. "Detective Moore. And you must be the stepbrother?"

"William Chanler. Lauren's stepbrother."

Nick's jaw tightened and then he moved across the kitchen to her. Before she could ask him what he was doing, he tipped her chin up and planted a heated kiss on her lips. "Good morning, babe."

Well, damn. Even though she knew it was for show only, she liked it. She really liked it. Hopefully, William would back off now. Nick was coming in handy at fending off men.

Nick faced William. "How long will you be staying here?" Nick asked.

"I'm not sure."

"How lucky for us." Nick's tone indicated his true feelings. He walked over and poured the rest of the coffee into a cup. Then he leaned back against the counter.

"I'd like to hear more about this ransacking. Which rooms exactly were hit?"

Nick nodded. "I'll get to that. First, where were

you on October thirty-first?"

William frowned. "At work, of course."

Nick nodded. "Is there someone who can corroborate that?"

Lauren coughed to hide her laugh. The light bulb must have gone on in William's head, because his expression changed. "Are you accusing me of something, Detective?"

Nick shrugged. "I have to question everyone."

William sneered as he stood up. "Did you question Lauren? You know she's not as innocent as she seems. I found that out last night," he said right before he left the room.

Lauren shuddered. "Ick. I think I'm going to be sick."

"Has he ever laid a hand on you?" Nick growled.

"No." She shuddered again. "He creeps me out. I've never stayed here with him alone. I'm glad you're here, Nick."

His eyes snapped to her and held her gaze. "I'm glad too. If he tries anything, let me know."

Plopping down in a chair, she studied him. "What would you do?"

Nick sat across from her. "I'd beat his ass."

"Is that part of your job, Detective?" Her lips curved up.

He leaned back in the chair and folded his arms, making his biceps bulge. She couldn't help but stare. She was human, after all. But when her eyes moved up, she saw that arrogant smirk.

"No, it's not part of my job. But it *is* part of my plan."

She quirked a brow. "Plan?"

He smiled and holy hell if his smile didn't light up the room. How had she not noticed he had dimples? And his teeth were perfect.

"My plan to get you to beg for something more than friendship. Because, make no mistake, Ms. Harrow, you will."

If she'd had anything other than her precious coffee in her hands, she would've thrown it at him.

"In your dreams, Moore." How dare he presume he could get her to beg. Although as her eyes raked over his chest one more time, she thought maybe he could.

The thud of a stack of papers dropping in front of her startled her. "It's in there," William said, moving to stand behind her.

She glanced down to see "Estate of Michael Chanler" across the front of the top page.

"*What's* in there?" she asked.

"The trust states you have the right to live in this house, but it does not allow you the right to have houseguests. Didn't you read the damn thing?"

She grabbed the document, stood up, and threw it at him. Papers went everywhere.

"No, I haven't read it." She'd received a copy of

the trust documents for his house but hadn't been able to look over them yet. She guessed that's what this was. She knew she should deal with it but then everything would be final. Her mom's death would be final. She wasn't ready to go there yet. "And this man is not a houseguest!" She was shouting now. She'd had enough of both men. "He's a damn detective here to protect us."

"A detective you said you were dating."

"That's right."

"According to Scott, you're sleeping with him, which brings me back to the fact he's not welcome here!"

Her brows shot up. "According to Scott?"

William held up his phone. "It's all over social media."

That was all she could stand of William for one day. She stormed out of the room and up the stairs. If William said one more word, she was really going to lose her shit.

A few moments later, there was a knock on her door. "It's Nick."

"Come in."

He walked in and stared at her lying on her bed. When his eyes turned molten, her worries over William melted away. She sat up and tried to sound casual. "What's up?"

He cleared his throat. "I have to go into work, but I don't like leaving you alone with him. Do you have a shift today?"

She shook her head. "No, but I'll be fine. I don't think he'd try anything until he has a few drinks in him."

Nick shoved his hands in his pockets. "Is he a day drinker?"

She laughed. "No. But he'll definitely have a few tonight. Any chance you want to stay another night?"

He grinned. "See, look at that. I've already got you asking me to stay."

She threw her pillow at him. "Stop."

He caught it and threw it back. "Seriously, I'll be here right after my shift."

Relief washed over her. As much as he might drive her nuts, she did feel safe when he was around.

"Hey."

Her eyes met his.

"If you need me today, call, okay?"

"Okay."

He held her gaze a little longer and then he slipped out of her room. His concern and that smoldering gaze had her heart fluttering. That reminded her, she needed to set up a night out with Harmony ASAP. The sooner she relieved her dry spell, the sooner she would stop reacting to Nick.

After Nick left, Lauren wandered out to the living room. She'd never seen anyone actually sitting in this room other than her, but the natural lighting was great for reading. She'd just gotten comfortable on the couch when William found her.

"I've been thinking about that ransacking." He sat on the coffee table across from her.

She set her book down. Wearing jeans and a sweater, William was dressed more casually than she was used to seeing him. His usual neat hair was a bit long. The purple under his eyes appeared to be fading to a greenish color.

"Did you hear what I said?" His voice had grown louder, and she realized she had no idea what he was talking about.

"No, sorry. I was looking at your eyes again. You told me you were tired, but there's no mistake you were in a fight. What happened?"

He stood and stepped away. "I was mugged. That's why I came here. I can't have my employees seeing me like this." He motioned to his face.

"Then why lie to me about it last night? You knew I'd see you today."

He shrugged. "Honestly, I'm embarrassed. But it's a good thing it happened."

She sat up. "How can you say that?"

"I thought I was invincible. Now I know I'm not. But back to what I was saying." He sat down on the coffee table again. "I'm not going to be here very long, and this house is really secluded. I think you should find a place in town. You know, that's safer. Especially since whoever came here could come back."

She picked her book up. There was no point to this conversation. If she'd had options, she wouldn't be here. "I'll be fine. I can't afford to go anywhere else anyway. That's why I'm here."

William clapped his hands. "Well, why didn't you say so? I'll help you out. Think of it as an early Christmas present."

"What are you saying?"

"You find a place and I'll pay the first six months' rent."

She frowned.

"Hell, I'll pay the first year's rent."

She crossed her arms. "Aside from this visit, you've seen me twice in the last year. First, your July fourth visit that you spent with friends and second, the funeral. Tell me, William, why are you so concerned about me now?"

"Well, someone needs to look out for you. You obviously blew through your inheritance."

"What are you talking about? What inheritance?"

William's face paled. "I'm so sorry. I thought my dad would have left you something. I missed the will reading and assumed you received some money."

"Nope."

"Hey, I have a house in town. You can stay there for as long as you like."

"You have a house in town? Since when?"

He shrugged. "I bought it a few years ago as an investment."

"Then why don't you stay there instead of here?"

He wore a deer in the headlight's expression. He rubbed his nose and smiled. "I've had renters until recently."

Her bullshit meter was going off.

"Why don't you send me the address and I'll think about it?"

"Sounds good. It's a nice place. You'll love it." He clapped his hands on his legs, then stood up and left. She didn't know William well, but she knew him well enough to know nothing about that conversation made sense.

Chapter Fourteen

William

William pounded on the door of Grace's house. His eyes scanned the overgrown bushes. The siding needed a fresh coat of paint. God, he could never live in a hellhole like this. The door whipped open.

"What is so urgent?" Grace glared at him.

William pushed past her inside. "How the hell does Lauren not know about the trust?"

Grace smiled. "Why don't you sit down? I'll make us something to drink."

He paced the room. The interior was in as bad of shape as the outside. He never understood why his aunt chose such a modest house. She was a Chanler, for God's sake. She had the means to live much better than this.

"Don't you look around my house like that."

He stopped pacing. "Like what?"

"Like it isn't good enough. Your face is scrunched as if you've smelled rotten eggs. It doesn't suit you."

He ran his hand through his hair. He never understood his aunt. She was different than he or his dad had been. Had never been interested in the corporation. All she ever cared about was her garden and all her plants.

Of course, even if she had been interested in the family business, his dad wouldn't have agreed to let her work there. William had no idea what happened between his dad and aunt, but he never saw them speak. It was always through someone else. Maybe now that his dad was gone, she'd be open to talking about it. But first, he had to get on her good side. He saw his opening when the greenhouse outside the window caught his eye.

"You know, I love your garden."

That lit her up. "Yes, and that greenhouse you got me a few years ago was a godsend."

"I'm glad you like it." He stared at it for a few seconds, then added, "Looks empty."

"It's nearly winter. Of course, it's empty. But I love it. Come sit." She patted one of the chairs at the dining room table. "Now, you asked about Lauren."

He sat down and a steamy cup of hot chocolate was on the table waiting for him.

"Wow, thank you. I can't remember the last

time I had hot chocolate."

He took a sip and made a face.

"It's dark chocolate."

He licked his lips. "Yes, it is. As for Lauren, she mentioned that she's broke. How can that be?"

Grace set her drink aside and clasped her hands together.

"To answer your question, Lauren doesn't know. She didn't go to the will reading and I understand she hasn't read her copy. I asked her once, but she said she wasn't ready. She needs some time."

"Time?" He cocked a brow.

"Well, I do plan to talk to her about it soon."

"She'll find out eventually and if I don't tell her, it will look like I'm trying to trick her." He ran his hands through his hair. He needed her out of the house, but it had to be her own choice.

"You know she'll turn thirty on Christmas Eve."

That got his attention. "Her birthday's on Christmas Eve?"

Grace nodded.

He took a long sip of the hot chocolate. "That's odd."

"Something wrong with your drink?"

He shook his head. "No, not that. I meant Lauren's birthday. My dad and her mom went on a holiday cruise each year. I thought it was a bit cold that they skipped being here for Christmas, but I was usually working, so I was busy anyway. But why would they skip out on her birthday too?"

Grace shrugged. "From what I knew of Candy, she viewed Lauren as an independent woman. She said many times that Lauren had her own life with Scott."

"What happened with her and Scott?"

Grace shrugged again. "He wants her back, but she doesn't want him."

"Huh." If she were with Scott, she'd probably leave town. That would be good for everyone.

"If you don't tell Lauren about the trust, I'll come out looking like the bad guy." He stood up. "You know what? I'm heading to the mansion now. I'll tell her when I get there." He finished the last of his drink in one gulp.

Grace stared up at him. "No."

He swallowed a laugh. "No? I'm afraid you can't tell me no. I'm not a child."

The smile she gave him chilled his blood. "No, you're not a child. But as you know, the trust only allows Lauren to stay in the home. Tell her and you're out."

Shit, she was right. He needed to tread carefully. "Why would that bother me? I could go back home or simply stay in the hotel in town."

She continued to stare at him. His heart began racing and sweat formed above his brow.

"I've heard rumors about you from the board

members."

He was breathing too fast. He was going to pass out. Slowly in—one, two, three. Out—one, two three. He tried to calm himself, and then he continued. "You know those board members have always had it in for me. I wouldn't believe anything they say."

"Are you telling me you aren't having financial problems?"

Shit. How would the board know that?

He pulled at the collar of his sweater. He was probably all sweaty. He was the worst liar in the history of liars. Damn, he was textbook for having all the tells. He took a deep breath and looked her directly in the eye. "No, I'm fine. Thank you for your concern."

He'd turned to leave when Grace called out to him. "I'm serious. Don't tell Lauren. I will. She'll take it better coming from me."

"All right. But do it soon," he said, and now he was burning up. He had to get out of there.

When he made it to his car, he yanked his sweater off and tossed it into the passenger seat. Thankfully, he'd put on a T-shirt underneath. Damn, maybe he was getting sick. His heart raced in his chest. It wasn't a cold, maybe it was his blood pressure. He'd left his medication in Portland when he'd come out here in a rush. He thought about calling in a refill but what if they could track him that way?

No, he'd be fine without it for a little while.

On the drive back to the mansion, he couldn't shake the fact that Lauren didn't know about her money. If she knew, she'd leave the house. Then he could have it all to himself. But he couldn't tell her about it without also telling her about the house. He slammed his fist on the steering wheel. *Damn it!*

His phone buzzed from his pants pocket. He pulled into the grocery store parking lot, and when he read the caller ID, he braced himself.

"Hey."

"Your check bounced."

He grimaced. "Yeah, I know. I'm sorry."

"I'll be at your condo in an hour. You'll pay me then."

A wave of nausea hit him hard. He had to stop this. "No, I'm not there."

"Where the hell are you?"

His heart slammed in his chest. "Look, Carl, I don't have your money yet. It's taking a little longer than I thought, but I'll have it by the end of the year."

"End of the year?!" the man barked from the phone. "That's nearly two months away! Why do you think I'd wait that long and not come and take care of you myself?"

William grabbed a bottle of water from the back seat and chugged it down. The cool liquid was soothing.

"You want your money and if I'm dead you

won't get it. Look you know where I live and work. I'm not going anywhere. Just give me this time and I'll make everything right."

Carl chuckled. "All right. This one time. But only because I know you're good for the added twenty percent late fee you'll be paying as well."

The man ended the call. William leaned back and counted his breaths to calm himself. He'd never gotten that worked up before. He needed to end this before he gave himself a damn heart attack.

"Damn you, Dad!" he shouted. If only his dad had left him something more than those fucking cars, he wouldn't be in this mess. Actually, no, it was his own fault. He'd done such a great job letting everyone think he'd made millions on his own that his dad didn't leave him any money. Instead he left it to a girl too stupid to know she was rich. What kind of person doesn't read the damn will?

Maybe she'd heard Michael saying that he was giving everything to the Red Cross on repeat, like he had. That had always been his plan. Well, until he married Candy Harrow. And now, that woman's daughter had a right to claim a house that was rightfully William's. He'd find a way to get it, though. Then sell it. He had to. He knew what Carl did to men who didn't pay.

Chapter Fifteen

After Nick heard Scott had been by the diner bothering Lauren, he convinced her they needed to have a public date night to get Scott to back off. Although he had a bad feeling nothing would make Scott back off. Based on what he'd heard around town, this guy had been given what he wanted since birth. And that was how Nick found himself standing on her doorstep holding a ridiculous Christmas wreath. He'd thought about flowers, but since Scott brought those last time, he didn't want her mind on Scott at all. He was still wearing what he'd worn all day. If this had been a real date, he would have gone home and changed. But that wasn't really possible when he was living in the same house as his date. Besides, he wanted to make sure William got the message too.

He'd asked the chief about William, but all his boss did was gush about the Chanler family. When Nick suggested he run a quick background check, the chief said no. No one investigates that family.

That didn't sit right either. Fortunately, he had a buddy from his old job who he could ask. Unfortunately, that buddy, Dillon, was on a two-week leave. He'd have to find an excuse to continue to stay at the mansion to watch over Lauren. But he'd worry about that later. Right now, he had a date.

He rang the bell and Lauren opened the door. Her eyes widened as she took in the wreath.

"This is for you." He held it up. "It seemed more festive than what your douche ex tried to give you."

"Wow. Thank you. A beautiful wreath and a shot at my ex. What more could a girl want?" She was smiling from ear to ear, and he swelled with pride that he'd put that smile there.

The realization that he wanted to put a smile on her face twisted his stomach. That kiss, her smile. Damn, he liked her. He'd gotten to know her enough to realize his initial impression of her had been wrong. She wasn't the rich princess he'd thought she was. She'd grown up differently than William.

"Where did you get a wreath so early in the season?"

He shrugged. "I know a guy." He wasn't going to mention he had it specially made, because this was supposed to be a fake date.

"Thank you. I hope I'm dressed all right. I didn't realize this was going to be so formal." She eyed his suit.

"No, you're fine. This is what I wore to work."

She smiled. "Of course."

"Let me hang this up."

They both turned to the door and he searched but found no hook.

"There's nothing to hang it on," Nick said.

"The Chanlers were never big on decorating. I bet there's never been a wreath on this door."

He frowned.

"We can put it up later."

"Oh, I can do that after you leave." An older woman was suddenly in the entryway. "Is this the detective I've heard so much about?"

"Yes. Grace, this is Nick. Nick, this is my stepaunt, Grace."

"Oh, you don't need to say step. We're family." Grace put her arm around Lauren's shoulders and gave her a squeeze. Then she held her hand out to Nick to shake.

"Nice to meet you. You really are a handsome man, aren't you?"

"Grace," Lauren warned.

Grace laughed. "Do you kids want to have happy hour here before you head out?"

Lauren looked at Nick.

"No, thank you. We have a reservation we need to get to."

"All right then. Have fun." Grace took the wreath from Lauren and walked toward the kitchen.

William appeared on the stairs behind Lauren and didn't even try to hide the scowl on his face.

"Before we head out for our date, I have to do one thing," Nick told her.

"What's that?" she asked.

He leaned in and brushed his lips against hers. She stilled in his arms but then melted into him. When he pulled back, he saw the same heat in her eyes that he felt. And William's scowl had only deepened.

"Let's go." He held out his arm and she took it.

They rode most of the way to the restaurant in silence.

"Why did you kiss me?" Lauren asked. "I thought this was a fake date."

He bit back his smile. If he'd told her this was a real date, she never would have agreed to it.

"William was on the stairs behind you. I hope he's starting to get the message."

"Oh." She sounded disappointed. Or was that just what he wanted? Time to find out.

"And I wanted to."

She turned to him. "You wanted to?"

He parked the car in the lot and faced her.

"I had to know if that last kiss was a fluke."

She grinned. "Or the one before that? And

what did you determine?"

He pushed some of her loose hair behind her ear. "That while you drive me nuts, I can't deny the pull I feel toward you. Tell me you feel it too."

"I do. I'm sorry I misjudged you at first. I thought you were an arrogant, self-involved dickhead."

"Wow."

"Oh, please. You didn't like me either."

He leaned in and kissed her neck. "But I still thought you were hot." His lips trailed up to her ear and she let out a moan. "Apparently, you only like me from the neck down."

She slapped his arm. "You know I didn't mean that."

"Are you sure? Because I've caught you staring several times now and not at my face." He kissed down her neck again.

She shivered. "We better get inside and have dinner before we get carried away."

"All right. But you should know, I don't sleep with anyone on the first date, so I'm not worried."

She threw her head back and laughed. "Good to know."

Once they had each been honest, the animosity melted away. They spent dinner talking and getting to know each other better. The more he learned, the more he liked. Lauren was a strong woman who wasn't worried about holding back her opinion. It was refreshing. Most people were intimidated by Nick and agreed to whatever he wanted. Not Lauren.

On the way back to the house, Nick had a smile plastered on his face. He couldn't remember when he'd had such a good time with someone. It even made the food taste better. Lauren was nothing like his ex, thank God.

"Are you going to walk me up to the door?" she asked.

"I am. Then I'm going to sneak into my room because I don't want to deal with William trying to kick me out. Nothing will ruin tonight."

"I'm sorry about him. I don't know why he was so rude to you."

Nick snorted. "I know exactly why he was rude to me. Do you think he'll be home when we get there?"

He drove up the driveway and spotted William's car still parked next to the house.

"Yep, looks like it. I still don't know why he's here," Lauren said.

Nick parked the car but neither of them got out.

"Why don't you ask him?" Nick asked.

Her gaze jerked to meet his. "I try not to talk to him, but I am curious. All these years he's been too busy running Chanler Enterprises to come home more than once a year. Why now?"

"Maybe he's grieving too."

She arched a brow. "I don't think I ever saw him show any affection toward Michael."

She turned to look at his car again.

"What's your gut telling you?"

"My gut?" she asked.

"Mm-hmm. Your gut. When I'm stuck on a case, I see where my gut leads me. Nine times out of ten, it's right."

She stared at him.

"What?"

"You're not what I expected."

He smiled. "Neither are you."

Lauren leaned back and took a deep breath. "All right. My gut tells me he's here because I'm here. This house sat empty for months and then shortly after I moved in, both Grace and William showed up and have some reason to stay here too. They both have their own houses in town."

"They do?"

"Yes. Grace said she's having her house renovated and it isn't ready yet. She recently returned from a cruise, and they were supposed to complete the project while she was gone. I guess they're running behind."

"Grace started staying here after you?"

"Yes, her first night was the night of the burning shit, but she said she came in through the garage and didn't see anything."

"And you're just now telling me about this?"

"I'm usually too busy arguing with you. It slipped my mind."

His head fell back against the car seat. Damn, this woman. He should be angry, but he wasn't. He couldn't be. Not when he wanted to kiss her again.

"All right. Well, what's wrong with William's house?"

"That's the weird thing. I had no idea he had a house in town, but the other day, he offered it to me, saying it was safer than staying here."

"Then why isn't he there?"

"That's what I wondered, so I asked him. He said he had renters in it until recently. My gut told me he was lying, but I can't prove it. He kept going on that it was safer than here."

"Safer than living here with a detective?"

She tilted her head. "As far as he's concerned, you've left."

Now it was his time to laugh. "Because he said so?"

She nodded.

"Do you have the address for William's house? I'd like to check out his story."

"I do. I'll text it to you before I go to bed."

Great. Now all he could picture was her in bed in the room next to him.

"Speaking of bed, we should go inside," Lauren said as she opened her door and got out.

Damn, he'd managed to kill the mood by

discussing the case.

They walked up to the house and Nick followed her up the porch steps. She was almost to the top step when the railing gave way and she stumbled. His arm went around her waist, righting her, and they stood close for several beats recovering from the near accident.

"Thank you. I almost fell."

He reluctantly released her and bent down to look at the long piece of wood that was lying on the ground.

The bottom of it had multiple screw holes and there was only one screw that was still attached. His eyes searched for the others, but it was too dark to see.

"That's strange. I use that railing all the time and I never noticed it was loose before." Lauren said.

"It appears it wasn't screwed down." But why would someone remove the screws? The top stair was seven steps up. Was someone intentionally trying to hurt her?

"I guess no one's really keeping up on the maintenance anymore." Lauren said. "I'll ask Grace about that."

He surveyed the property as best he could with only the house lights and moonlight. The grass was short, likely last mowed the previous month, before the morning frosts became a regular event. Despite the large, bare trees that spanned the property, there were no leaves on the ground. This house was not being neglected. His gut told him the loose railing was something else entirely.

"You coming?" Lauren's voice cut him out of his thoughts.

He spun to face her. She'd made it to the front door.

"Yes, don't go in yet."

He took the steps two at a time and then was in front of her.

"Why not?"

"Because that's not how real dates end. Well, not unless they've gone really bad."

She sucked in her bottom lip. "When you first suggested this date, I thought it was a date for show. A fake date for our fake relationship," she whispered. "But something changed."

He moved closer, and they were almost touching. When her breath hitched, he couldn't hold back his grin.

"Does this feel fake to you?"

She shook her head. One of his hands reached for her waist and pulled her to him, closing the remaining distance between them, while the other went to the back of her head, keeping it steady as he leaned in and pressed his lips to hers.

"Does this feel fake?"

"No."

He kissed from her jaw to her ear, and her arms went around his neck.

"Good, because it's not. I want to take you out again this weekend."

"I'd like that," Lauren said, smiling.

His lips finally met hers, brushing gently at first, and then he slipped his tongue in and deepened the kiss. Her hand moved under his button up, roaming up to his bare chest. When she let out a little moan, he pulled away before he lost control and took her up against the door.

"Good night, Ms. Harrow. Sweet dreams." They were both breathing hard.

"Good night, Detective."

She opened the door and he followed her in. He let her go ahead of him and up the stairs. If he got too close, he might not be able to go into his own room.

Her hips swayed with each step as he trailed her to the top, and then he watched her go into her bedroom. Before he made it into his own room, he heard a man's angry voice coming from somewhere down the hall. William. Walking lightly so as not to make any sound, he found himself in front of William's door.

"I'm doing everything I can!" William yelled.

Nick could hear a faint muffled voice. He must be on the phone.

"She needs to leave the house on her own. I can't throw her out."

After a pause, he added, "I don't have that

right. You have to trust me on this; I'll get her out. It's taking a little longer than I thought."

William let out a long sigh.

"A week? No, I can't do... Hello? Shit!"

Then there was a loud crash. Nick quickly made his way back to his room. His gut told him Lauren's stepbrother was behind the ransacking. That would explain why nothing had actually been taken. The plan had been to scare Lauren into leaving the house. But why? Why would he care that she was staying here? What he also had to figure out was whether Grace was in on it too.

Chapter Sixteen

Lauren yawned as she walked into the kitchen.

"Good morning." Grace was sitting at the table holding on to her cup of coffee.

"Good morning. I didn't realize you stayed here last night."

"I didn't want you waking up alone on Thanksgiving."

"Happy Thanksgiving. I can't believe I only have to work a half shift today. We could cook up something easy tonight. I forgot to buy a turkey." Lauren grabbed her favorite World's Best Accountant mug from the cabinet. Then she pulled out the coffee pot, only to realize it was empty.

Grace stood up. "Oh, sorry. I wasn't sure if anyone else drank coffee. I can make some more."

"No, I can do it."

Lauren got out everything she needed to make the coffee, and while she waited for it to brew, she noticed Grace was staring at her.

"Is anything wrong?" Lauren asked.

"Oh no, not at all. There's something I want to talk to you about."

"Sounds serious."

Grace took a swallow of her coffee. "No, it's just that it looks like William packed up and left and I have plans this weekend. I'll be gone through Sunday. I'm sorry we didn't arrange a get-together for the holiday."

Lauren turned, not wanting her aunt to see the disappointment on her face. Apparently, her days of celebrating the holidays were behind her. She pulled the coffee pot out, poured enough to fill her cup, then put it back to continue brewing.

"That's fine. I'll relax and catch up on my reading," she said as she took a seat at the table with Grace.

Nick walked into the kitchen. "There's no big Thanksgiving feast planned?"

"Nope. No surprise there." Lauren couldn't keep the sarcasm from her voice. "I just started a pot of coffee."

"Thank you."

This was the first morning she could remember that he'd come down fully dressed.

Actually, it was the first morning she'd seen him in weeks. The morning after their date, Nick talked to William and Grace about the railing that gave way. He convinced them that someone was trying to harm one of them. They then agreed it would be best for Nick to stay there for the time being, in his own room, of course. Living with the equivalent of two parents was a serious drag.

Although it probably didn't matter since she'd hardly seen Nick much anyway. With the holiday season in full swing, Logan had needed her to work extra hours at the diner, and she was grateful for the extra money. And Nick had been called out nearly every night for the past couple of weeks on crazy calls. Seriously, how many times could goats get loose? They hadn't made it out for a second official date yet, but the couple of evenings they did get to spend together, she'd gotten to know Nick even better. At this point, he was looking less like a rebound guy and more like a man she could really fall for.

"Did I hear you say William packed up and left?" Nick asked Grace.

She nodded. "Yes, he must have gone back to Portland."

"He didn't mention to you he was leaving?"

Grace laughed. "No, he doesn't tell anyone much of anything. When I walked past his room this morning, the door was wide open, and his bags were gone."

"What about all those boxes he had delivered?"

"They're still there. Detective, do you always question everything?" Grace wore a smile.

He chuckled. "I guess I do."

"Well, it's my turn now," Grace said and turned to Lauren. "Scott's pushing his story again that you cheated on him with Nick. What are you going to do about it?" Grace brought her coffee to her lips.

"Why would he do that? It's been weeks. That damn story finally died down. I thought everyone knew I didn't cheat."

"I know you didn't." Grace set her cup down and folded her hands. "I'm trying to figure out why half the town thinks you two" — she gestured between Lauren and Nick — "are a couple. It's obvious you're not. I never see you together. And I don't hear either of you sneaking into the other's room."

"We're new. We're not at the sneaking into each other's room's stage," Nick said hoarsely.

Grace waved her hand. "You're both young and attractive. If you aren't ripping each other's clothes off yet, you have no business dating."

Nick choked on his coffee. "You hear that, Lauren? We should be ripping each other's clothes off." He smiled as he coughed. "Maybe that's what we should be doing when Grace and William discover us during those few moments we get together."

Those damn dimples of his were on full

display, and great, now she was picturing him naked while she was in the same room as her aunt.

Based on his heated stare, Nick was thinking the same thing.

"Besides, I'm not the only one who's noticed. The other half of the town thinks you lied to make an easy break from Scott," Grace continued.

Lauren laughed. "Easy? There's been nothing easy about Scott."

"That's probably true, but I talked to him yesterday. He's got his hopes up that this is a lie and he can win you back."

Lauren stood. "He needs to leave me alone. I want him out of my life."

Nick was immediately at her side, wrapping her in his arms. She eased into his chest and inhaled his intoxicating scent.

"We need to be more public about our dating, so he gets the message," he said. Then he pulled back and kissed her forehead. God, she wanted more of him, but it shouldn't be as a show for someone else.

"We shouldn't have to," she said.

He released her from his embrace and studied her as if he was trying to get a read on her.

"I know what you two can do." Grace was grinning. "The ice rink will start running tomorrow. Go. Have fun."

"Ice skating?" Lauren asked. She'd heard the town made a big deal of the holidays, but since she only visited during the summers, she'd never been around this time of year.

"That sounds perfect. Thank you, Grace," Nick said as he sat at the table.

"It does?" Lauren was shocked Nick would agree to it. His bulky frame alone must make it difficult to skate.

"I see that look in your eye." He smiled at her. "I'll have you know I can get around the ice quite well."

Her mouth fell open. "I can't picture you figure skating."

He burst out laughing. "Neither can I. But I did play hockey now and then as a teenager, and I started up again when I got out of the service."

"You were in the service?"

"I was. Army. Tell me, where is this ice rink? I haven't seen one when I've driven around town."

"How did I not know you were in the service?"

Nick winked at her. "There's a lot about me you don't know yet."

Her gaze swept up his body as she imagined him in uniform. "Do you still have your uniform?" Her voice came out huskier than she'd intended.

His eyes darted to hers. The corners of his mouth curled up. "Got a thing for guys in uniform, do you?"

Telltale warmth spread up her neck and she

turned to the coffee maker.

"Grace, tell us more about this ice rink." She pretended to fiddle with the carafe, hoping her aunt would take her cue. No such luck.

Then Nick was behind her. So near that his chest was up against her back, his lips at her ear. "I have another uniform you might like—well, it's more of a suit."

He couldn't mean that, could he? Damn it. She was picturing him naked again.

"That's what I'm talking about," Grace said, fanning herself.

Lauren spun to face Nick and they were so close; any stranger would think they were about to kiss.

"I don't know what you mean, Grace. I was referring to my department dress blues."

He winked at Lauren and her cheeks grew hotter. Damn it again.

"Isn't that what you were imagining me wearing, Ms. Harrow?"

Heat emanated from his hooded eyes, and she wanted to rip his shirt off and show him what she was imagining.

"I take back what I said. If you two have even half of this chemistry out in public, no one will doubt a thing. Damn." Grace continued fanning herself.

Lauren needed to get this conversation under control. Being this close to Nick was unnerving.

Chasing Her Trust

Pushing past him, she put some space between them. "Let's get back to the topic of the ice-skating rink. Tell us about it, Grace."

Grace's face lit up. "Oh, it's seasonal. They set it up in the town park. It lasts through January. Draws quite a crowd at times." Grace clapped her hands together. "It's settled then. I'm going to call my friend and ask him to go too. I can't wait to see you two out on the ice."

Lauren's stomach clenched. She'd never been on ice skates in her life. Making an idiot of herself in front of Nick was not high on her to-do list.

"Wait. I'm sure Nick has plans to be with his family this weekend. Maybe we'll go another time." Lauren smiled, happy to have found a way to get out of it.

"No plans for tomorrow night." Nick looked at her.

"You don't have any family in the area?"

"I do, but they're celebrating on Saturday."

"Wonderful! You're both free tomorrow night for ice skating." A huge grin broke out across Grace's face.

Lauren forced another smile. "Sounds good. I'll grab something from the diner after my shift for dinner tonight. Then ice skating tomorrow."

She had tried to sound convincing, but her nerves must have shown, because Nick wrapped her in his arms and whispered in her ear. "Don't worry. I won't let you fall."

Damn it, this man. She was already worried that it was becoming too late for that.

* * *

"Shoe size?" the man behind the counter asked.

"Seven."

He threw a pair of ice skates up on the counter and Lauren eyed them. She turned to look at the rink, watching everyone skate. Why did everyone know how to skate?

Nick grabbed both his and her skates. "C'mon." He walked to a nearby bench, then started to put his on.

She swallowed hard, knowing she had to tell him. It would be obvious when he was spinning circles around her.

She sat down and slowly put a skate on.

"Are you all right? You look like you might be sick."

Okay, this was her chance. "I'm nervous."

"No need to be nervous. Once everyone sees our chemistry, there'll be no doubt in anyone's minds we're together."

Together? Her stomach flipped. "Together?"

He leaned down and kissed her lightly.

"I know this started off fake, but I thought I made myself clear the night I took you to dinner. I like you, Lauren. I like you a lot. And I would have made that clearer, but we never have the house to ourselves."

With every word and every touch, he managed to inch a little more into her heart.

"Let's go." He grabbed her hand.

"Wait." It was now or never. "I wasn't talking about our chemistry. Although I really like you too and all of this has taken me by surprise. And at the moment, I really want to know what you mean by making things clearer, but—"

"I meant if we'd been alone, I would have shown you with every kiss." His lips were on her neck, nibbling it softly. "Every caress." His fingers stroked her cheek. "My lips and fingers would have shown you exactly how I feel. Repeatedly." His hand slipped down her back and cupped her ass, drawing her up against his body, where there was no mistaking his arousal.

She let out a small groan and he moved back.

"We should get on the ice now. I need to cool off." He winked and reached for her hand again.

"Nick, damn it, you can't do that and then expect me to think clearly. Give me a second."

He laughed. "There's no need to think clearly. We're just skating."

"That's the problem. I'm nervous because I've

never ice skated."

There, she said it.

His jaw fell open. "Really? You've never been to this rink? I thought everyone who lived here made a point of coming here." The surprise fell from his face and was replaced with understanding. "But you said you were only here during the summers."

Turning away, she swallowed down the sadness that came over here. "Yes, never for the holidays."

His finger lifted her chin back to him. "You never came here even for a short visit for the holidays?"

She shook her head. "Once my mom married Michael and moved here, she changed. I was in my last year of college and she told me they were taking a holiday cruise and wouldn't be home."

"For the entire holiday season? You didn't celebrate any of it with your mom at all? No Thanksgiving? No Christmas?"

She continued shaking her head. "Not after she married him. I only came here on summer break during college. Usually my mom came to me but never during the holidays."

His arms wrapped around her waist and he scooted her next to him. "Shit, Lauren. I'm sorry. That sounds lonely."

She laughed. "Yeah, it was. My mom told me to enjoy the extra time with Scott. I dated him through all of it."

Nick pulled back with a frown. "Wait, Scott's from Fisher Springs, right?"

"Well, his last name is Fisher."

"Didn't he invite you to spend the holidays with his family?"

She laughed. "Not once. We dated for six years and he never asked me to spend the holidays with him. He said his family only allowed spouses at their holiday gatherings, not girlfriends."

"Well, he's an idiot. If you were mine, I'd want to spend all my holidays with you."

"Stop. Don't pity me."

He laughed. "Are you always this stubborn?"

She stood up and put her hands on her hips. "Why the hell are you calling me stubborn?" Forgetting she'd put the skates on, she started to fall when her ankles wobbled.

Nick was up immediately and had her in his arms. He held her close, staring into her eyes as he spoke. "I don't pity you."

"I'm sorry. I'm a bit defensive after Scott."

"I understand. I was too after what happened with my ex."

"Your ex? Sounds like there's a story there."

He kissed her. "For another time. Let's go get you on the ice."

He helped ease her out onto the ice, her free hand flailing to keep her up. Snaking his arm around her waist, he moved them both forward, slowly at first, then he picked up a little more speed, so they'd at least pass the toddlers.

After a couple of times around, she felt comfortable enough to look at her surroundings. The low fence around the rink was decorated with Christmas lights and garlands. It really did look like a winter wonderland. But when her gaze moved up, that's when she noticed how many people were staring at them.

"We're being watched," she whispered.

"Well, we should give them what they want then."

She laughed. "Me falling on my ass?" She tightened her grip on his arm. "Wait, I was kidding. Don't let me go."

"I don't intend to."

She stole a glance at him. His gaze was intense. If only she could free a hand, she'd move it over his chiseled jaw before tracing down his strong pecs to his abs and then...

"You know you keep looking at me like that and I'll have to do something about it."

Her gaze found his and he winked.

"C'mon." Without loosening his grip on her, he managed to guide them to the center of the rink, where he spun around and started skating backward, holding her in front of him. Then he stopped them both.

"What are you doing? You're not going to fake propose, are you?"

"No, but that would certainly send a message."

He smiled and his dimples were on full display, obliterating her remaining self-control. Her hand threaded through his hair and she pulled him down for a kiss.

Chapter Seventeen

Several people were clapping and a few were whistling, but Nick didn't care. All he cared about in that moment was the woman in his arms who stared up at him through her long lashes. Every time he kissed her; he didn't think it could be better. But he was wrong.

"We should go," Lauren said, her eyes wide as she looked around.

"Not yet. I have something I want to ask you." He leaned down and brushed his lips against hers.

"I told you, don't fake propose."

"Please come to my family's Thanksgiving tomorrow."

Her gaze shot to his, but she didn't say anything.

"Don't overthink it," he whispered in her ear.

"What do you want to do?"

Her lips curved up. "I want to accept your invitation."

Those words made him happier than he'd expected. He wasn't sure how he'd become so drawn to her in such a short time.

"Good. We need to leave around noon tomorrow, which gives us plenty of time to enjoy this evening."

He bent down for another kiss.

"But I need to bring something. If we stop at the store tonight, I can grab what I need to make a pie in the morning."

"A pie?"

"Yes, I have to bring something. Does your mom like pumpkin pie?"

He pulled her close. This woman. "Yes, but I'm afraid I have to burst your bubble. Nothing tomorrow will be homemade."

She leaned back to look into his eyes. "What do you mean?"

He moved to the side and wrapped his arm around her waist again. "Let's get off the ice. I'll explain."

He guided her until they were part of the outer circle and then they stepped off the ice. After they turned in their skates and walked through the park, she stopped in front of him.

"What aren't you telling me?"

Those amber irises searched his, full of worry.

"It's no big deal. It's just that my parents don't cook. Dinner will be catered."

"Catered? Like those precooked meals you buy from the grocery deli? I thought of doing that once, but the smallest meals are usually made to serve a family."

He laughed. "Well, it won't come from the grocery store, but yes, it will be made by someone else."

Grabbing her hand, he pulled her toward the concession stand. "Want a hot chocolate?"

"Yes, thank you."

The smell of the chocolate, along with a hint of peppermint floated on the air. He'd never been out to Fisher Springs for their holiday festival but being here tonight with Lauren felt right. He could see doing this year after year with her.

Whoa. He took a step back, not prepared for that thought. The last time he'd considered something lasting was with his ex, and it had turned out to be a disaster. A disaster he relived every time he went home. His sister was still best friends with the woman. He'd never had the heart to inform her of what really happened. It would ruin their friendship.

"What aren't you telling me?" She watched him carefully as the barista whipped up their hot chocolates.

Damn. He normally was good at hiding his

emotions, but it was hard around her. Well, she was going to find out soon enough. He might as well rip off the Band-Aid.

"My parents have money, similar to the Chanlers. Any meal they serve is usually prepared by the best chef they can locate. My mother mentioned that dinner tomorrow would be prepared by their favorite restaurant."

"Two hot chocolates for Nick!" the barista called out.

He grabbed the cups off the counter and handed one to Lauren. Then his phone buzzed in his pocket.

"I need to check this in case it's the chief."

It wasn't. It was a message with the background check on William he'd been waiting on. Thankfully, when Dillon returned from leave, he'd been more than willing to help him out. He shoved the phone back in his pocket. Now wasn't the time to read it. He looked over at Lauren. She was watching the skaters.

"What are you thinking about?"

Her lips were pursed when she turned to him. "If I made a pie and took it, they wouldn't consider it good enough, right?"

He groaned. It was true. His parents were snobs. "Probably. I'm sorry. That's them. It's not me."

"Are you sure? Because you were pretty arrogant when I met you."

There was no smile on her face. She was being serious.

"What are you worried about, Lauren?"

"That you're going to decide I'm not enough." As she stared out at the rink, a tear dropped from her eye and ran down her cheek.

Nick sat down next to her and wiped it away. "I'm not Scott." Then she faced him, and he leaned his forehead against hers. "I really like you, Lauren. You like me too. You already admitted it." He grinned like a fool.

She laughed, and it was the sexiest sound he'd ever heard. "I'll admit you're growing on me."

"I knew it." He kissed her. "Let's go home and watch a movie."

Home. He liked that idea too much. He was falling hard for this woman.

★ ★ ★

Dropping Lauren off at her room last night was one of the hardest things Nick had done in a long time. He wanted her, and he could tell she wanted him. But he wasn't going to rush this. He needed to be sure he wasn't just her rebound. He hadn't felt like this about a woman since his ex, Samantha. And he wasn't even positive whether he'd really loved her or if their relationship had simply been convenient for everyone. She was his sister's best friend and their moms were also best friends.

That was why he hadn't told anyone what really happened. Of course, Sam hadn't helped matters by leading everyone to believe the breakup was his fault.

He did call it off after he discovered Sam in bed with her friend James. Her so-called friend she'd said she only thought of as a brother. The fact she'd told Nick that so many times should have clued him in. Then Sam had tried to sell him some story that it had been a one-time thing and she'd been lonely. Hell, she knew when he enlisted that he'd likely have long tours. She'd said she was fine with it. Turns out, she wasn't fine. But what really dug the knife into the wound further was when he found out James was poised to take over his family's business. In other words, the guy was loaded, and Sam was trying to move on. From what he heard from his sister, it worked. Until she caught James cheating on her. That's karma for you.

Since then, his mom and sister had been trying to get them back together. Never going to happen.

When they saw Lauren with him tomorrow, hopefully, they'd finally understand he'd moved on too. He'd moved on ten years ago, but they didn't seem to get that memo.

That was enough thinking about his ex. He needed to focus on the background report he'd received on William. William had been flagged in the system by a cop down in Oregon for associating with a convicted felon. Apparently, this felon was known for giving loans to gamblers, addicts — whoever was desperate enough to pay him back twice the rate. But as he read it, something didn't sit right. Why would William associate with him? He had plenty of family money. Unless he was the one backing the operation.

On Monday, he'd call his friend and that cop in Oregon to dig deeper.

* * *

With one last look in the mirror, he smirked as he took in his outfit. His parents wouldn't appreciate the jeans, but they'd grown used to it. The moment he moved out of their house; he gave up the designer clothes. He wore suits while on the job, but they certainly weren't designer. That wasn't something he could afford on his salary.

When he walked into the kitchen, Lauren was sitting at the table sipping tea. Before she realized he was there, he had a chance to really take her in. Her long blond hair was pulled into a ponytail at her neck and she wore a cream sweater that begged for his fingers to touch. She didn't wear jeans. No, she went with the more respectable black trouser. She was perfect.

Sensing his presence, she glanced up and smiled.

"Ready?"

"Sure am. Are you?" Grabbing her teacup, she took it to the sink then spun around, her hips swaying as she closed in on him.

He groaned. "You know that leaving you at your room last night, alone, was nearly impossible for me, don't you?"

She wrapped her arms around his neck. "Then why didn't you join me?"

"I'm trying to be a gentleman."

"I don't want a gentleman."

She leaned in and kissed him, and it quickly turned hot and heavy until he pulled back.

"All right. Tonight, you won't get a gentleman. But if we don't stop, we'll never get to my parents' house."

"Mmm. Something to look forward to. But you're right. We need to get going. Plus, we have to stop and get flowers."

He intertwined his fingers in hers and led her toward the door. "Already done. I went to the grocery store this morning and grabbed the biggest bouquet they had."

She squeezed his hand. "Thank you. I can't wait to meet your family. I bet they're so proud of you."

He opened his mouth to warn her, then

stopped. Maybe his parents would behave well in front of company. He could hope. He didn't think he could take another round of guilt because he didn't get a business degree.

Chapter Eighteen

As they drove into his parent's driveway, he stole a glance her way. Her eyes were huge as saucers.

"Um, Nick?"

The garage doors automatically opened, and he parked inside.

"Yes?" he asked.

"This is your parents' place? You grew up here?"

"I did."

"You mentioned you had money. Nick, this is beyond having money."

Was she interested in his money? Sam sure had been. Better find out fast.

"None of it's mine. When I refused to join the family company, my dad cut me off. He believes I'll come back begging for it."

She frowned. "I'm sorry. That must be hard."

He shook his head. "No. Actually, it's not. This isn't the life I wanted."

"It's good to know what you want. And what you don't want. It makes everything clear."

Well, that sounded mysterious. "Lauren, do you know what you want?"

The corner of her mouth curved up.

"There you are! Come inside, everyone's waiting on you," his sister called out, standing outside the car and staring at them. Of course, she had to ruin the moment. He swore she had radar for that sort of thing.

They got out of the car and he made his way around to Lauren's side.

"Lauren, this is my sister, Gwen. Gwen, this is Lauren."

Gwen's smile fell. "I didn't realize you were bringing a date. You never bring a date."

He turned back to Lauren. "Lauren's different. I wanted you all to meet her."

It was impossible not to notice Gwen wasn't happy with Lauren's presence. He knew his sister wanted him with Sam, but he hadn't thought she'd be outright rude.

"Let's go inside," he whispered to Lauren.

Once they were in the house, he understood his sister's reaction.

"Nick! You look great. Still working out I see," Sam said as she approached him. Her hands were immediately on his arm as she squeezed in what appeared to be her trying to show ownership. Why the hell was she here?

Untethering himself from Sam, he wrapped his arm around Lauren's waist. "Sam, I'd like you to meet Lauren. My date."

Sam jerked back. "Date?"

"Yes," Nick said firmly.

Lauren didn't miss a beat. She stepped forward and held out her hand. "Nice to meet you, Sam."

Fortunately, Sam was big on social graces, so she willingly took her hand and shook it. "Nice to meet you too."

Nick's mom appeared from around the corner. "Oh, Nick! I'm so glad you made it. And who is this?" She cocked her head as her gaze swept over Lauren. Her lips pursed into a straight line.

"Mom, this is Lauren. My girlfriend."

"Wait, your date or your girlfriend?" Gwen asked.

"Come on into the dining room. We're about to be served." His mother swiveled around without any more acknowledgment of Lauren and left the room. He and Lauren stood still until Gwen and Sam left too.

"Nick, what am I walking into?"

He pulled her into his arms. "I'm so sorry. I have no idea why Sam is here."

With her hands on his chest, she pushed until she broke from his grasp. "Who exactly is she?"

He let out a long sigh. "My ex."

"Oh."

"From ten years ago."

Her eyes grew wide. "Wow. Have you dated her since then?"

"No."

"Then why is she sniffing around you like she owns you? And your sister and mother didn't seemed thrilled I was here either. Did you tell them you invited me?"

When he looked at the floor, she hit his chest. "You didn't tell them?"

"I just invited you last night and there's always plenty of food. Sam hasn't eaten with us in years. I didn't expect this."

"And, obviously, they didn't expect me. Color us all surprised!"

Now he had four angry women to deal with. The odds of coming out of this alive were dwindling by the moment.

At least he only needed to make one happy.

"Lauren, I'll go ask Sam to leave. Then we can have a nice dinner."

Her hands went straight to her hips. "No, you will not. Clearly, she's an invited guest. I'm the intruder."

She tried to spin toward the door, but he caught her, his arms around her waist, her back to his chest. "You're not an intruder. You're my guest. Now let's go eat and make small talk."

"Sounds fun."

"If it gets to be too much, you can squeeze my hand and we'll leave. All right?"

She nodded. "All right."

By the time they made their way into the dining room, everyone was sitting down.

"Lauren, why don't you sit here by me?" His mother motioned to the chair next to her. Lauren cast a hesitant glance at Nick but then went to the chair and sat down.

That left one remaining chair that was next to Sam and a mile away from Lauren. She couldn't squeeze his hand if she wanted to.

"Oh! Nicky, come sit here."

God, he couldn't stand that nickname.

From the moment he sat down, Sam was constantly touching him. Mostly it was her leg rubbing on his under the table.

Two servers entered the room and brought in their dinner. It consisted of the traditional holiday fare—turkey, stuffing, mashed potatoes, and gravy. Then came a dish that only he liked. He was about to thank his mother for ordering it, but then Lauren spoke.

"Are those brussels sprouts? I love those." He could hear the excitement in her voice as she stared at the dish.

"It's my favorite." He grinned at her.

"Remember the time I made you brussels sprouts with bacon?" Sam ran her hand through his hair. "You said you could eat those off me all day."

"Stop it, Sam," Nick snapped.

"Oh, you know you used to love it when I played with your hair." She put her other hand on his chest. "I remember everything you love." Then her hand moved down below the table's surface.

Lauren frowned and tossed her napkin on her plate. "I'm sorry. I'm not hungry after all." She scooted away from the table and walked out of the room.

Nick stood up fast, causing his chair to fall back. "Wait, Lauren."

But she was already gone.

"Let her go. We need to talk," Sam said.

"No, we don't. You all have gone too far. The real reason Sam and I broke up and why I want nothing to do with her is because she cheated on me. Repeatedly."

His mother gasped and his sister's eyes widened. Nope, they hadn't known the truth.

"Now if you'll excuse me, I'm going to apologize to my girlfriend and hope I can make this right."

* * *

Lauren made it to the driveway and couldn't hold back the tears. How had she fallen so far, so fast with Nick? Watching his ex put her hands all over him was too much. And he didn't push her away. Why didn't he push her away? God, now she was standing here crying like a fool.

"Lauren!" Nick called from the doorway.

She froze. She should call an Uber, let him get back in there with Sam.

When she turned to him, he was right there.

"Nick, it's all right. We were only supposed to be fake. If you want her, that's fine. I'll call an Uber and head home."

"No. We're going home together."

She shook her head. "No, you can't walk out on your family like that."

"I'm not letting you go."

Confusion must have been written on her face.

"Look, Lauren, I'm sorry about what happened in there. I finally told them the truth, and hopefully, they'll stop trying to push Sam and me back together. But understand this, I have no interest in her. If I did, I would be with her. Understand?"

She nodded, unable to get any words out.

He wiped her tears away. "Lauren, I told you what I feel for you is real. And based on your reaction,

I think your feelings are real too."

She swallowed hard, then whispered, "They are."

He leaned down and kissed her lightly. "Let's go grab some takeout and head back. It sounds like we might have the house to ourselves tonight," he winked.

She laughed.

"Not quite the reaction I was aiming for, but I'm glad you're smiling now."

"You're not at all who I thought you were."

"That goes the same for you."

"My first impression was that you were this arrogant asshole, and then you blew me off when I found that burning dog doo on my porch. Why?"

He took a step back, shoving his hands in his pockets. "I'm not proud to say this, but I judged you. You can see what I grew up around. When I showed up at the mansion, I assumed you were one of them. Between the way you behaved in the store—"

"No, the store was all you."

He grinned. "Agree to disagree. Let's get out of here."

On the drive back, they stopped and picked up takeout. They didn't speak during the ride, so she took that time to mull over what had happened. What bothered her the most was her reaction. When Sam put her hands on Nick, Lauren was ready to throw knives at her. She wasn't a jealous person, yet she couldn't explain her reaction. She felt something for Nick. No doubt there. But exactly what and the depth of it scared her. She'd only known this man for a month. And most of that time, they hadn't liked each other.

Once they got to the mansion and went inside, she set plates on the kitchen table and he pulled the food out of the bags.

"Would you like some wine?" she asked.

His face scrunched up. "You happen to have beer?"

"Let me look." In the fridge, she found several bottles of dark beer. "Hope this will do." She set two of them by their plates.

"You've been quiet," Nick said as he popped the tops.

After a sip to fortify herself, she sat with him at the table. "I had a lot to think about."

"Like what?"

Well, might as well dive in. If he was going to run scared, now was his chance.

"My reaction to Sam today was stronger than I expected. It took me by surprise."

"Well, she is a lot to take." He unwrapped his burrito.

She pried back the lid on her taco salad. "That's not what I meant. I was fine until she put her hands on you."

He stopped mid-bite, his lips curving into a

smile. "You were jealous?"

She frowned. "Yes. But stop smiling. That's not a good thing."

"Why the hell not?"

"I'm not the jealous type. I don't like feeling out of control."

Immediately, he was out of his chair and kneeling next to her. "Every time I hear Scott is at the diner trying to see you, I see red. At first, it scared me too because, somehow, you've not only gotten under my skin, but you've also crept into my heart. I swore after Sam that I wouldn't let anyone else in. It didn't seem worth it." His hands were around her waist and he leaned closer. "And I can't say that with you, it was love at first sight, because we both know that's a lie."

She laughed. Her eyes were welling up again.

"I'm sorry. I'm not trying to upset you." He wiped away the tears that fell.

"No, it's not that. They're happy tears."

"Happy to hear I'm falling for you, Lauren? Cause I am. And as much as you didn't like feeling jealous, I have to say that hearing you might feel even a little close to what I'm feeling makes me a very happy man."

Nick wasn't anything like her ex at all. The final wall to her heart was crumbling down.

His lips brushed hers lightly, but she needed more. Placing her hands on his shoulders, she pulled him closer and deepened the kiss.

When his tongue swiped hers, she let out a little moan. Then he pulled back and stood up, breathless. "We should finish dinner because if we keep going, I'm not going to want to stop."

She stood as well, hugging his waist. "I don't want to stop. I want you, Nick. All of you."

Chapter Nineteen

"I don't want to stop. I want you, Nick. All of you."

Those words were his undoing. His mouth was instantly on hers again. When he lifted her under her legs, she wrapped them around him, and without breaking their kiss, he carried her up to his bedroom, kicking the door closed behind him.

Nick gently lowered her to the floor, and when their lips parted, he searched her face. "Are you sure?"

She smiled. "For a detective, you really don't pick up on all the signs, do you?"

He groaned. "Do you have any idea how much that smart mouth of yours turns me on?"

"Show me."

He flipped them around so that her back was against the door. "Take your hair down," he ordered.

Her eyes darkened. She liked his demand.

Chasing Her Trust

Never taking her gaze off him, she pulled her hair free and it swung around her shoulders. Then his fingers wove through it as his mouth crushed down on hers.

Lauren ran her palms under his T-shirt and up his back. "Take this off," she said against his lips, and he grabbed the hem and yanked it off, tossing it to the floor. Her eyes roamed his chest, and his heart beat faster at her appreciative gaze.

"I've been wanting to touch you in this sweater all day." He leaned in and kissed a trail up her neck while his hand moved under her sweater until he cupped her breast. His thumb lightly stroked her pebbled nipple through her bra.

She moaned and he stroked harder as she raked her nails down his back and found the top of his jeans. When she went to unbutton them, he stopped her. "Wait. We're focusing on you first."

He pulled her sweater up and she took the hint and finished removing it. At the sight of her black lacy bra, he nearly swallowed his tongue. And when she slowly undid the button of her pants and tugged them off, he had to adjust himself. Her creamy skin against the black lace was sexy as hell. But then another thought struck him.

"Lauren, did you wear lacy black underwear to meet my parents?"

She eased toward him again. "Do you really want to talk about your parents right now?" But before he could answer, she wrapped her arms around his neck and kissed him hard.

Grabbing her ass, he picked her up and she threw her legs around him. He took a few steps forward and placed her on the bed, his lips traveling down her neck while his fingers quickly unhooked her bra. *Thank God for front clasps.* Taking a nipple into his mouth, he flicked one and then the other as she groaned.

"Nick, I need to touch you. Please take off your clothes."

"Soon." He unbuttoned the top of his jeans to provide some relief. Seeing her on his bed had made him painfully hard.

Skimming his hand up her thigh, he found his way to those lacy panties. Damn, they were soaked through. "You're so wet for me." He lightly traced his fingers over the damp fabric, teasing her. Her hips bucked, trying to get more contact.

"I've been wet for you since you lent me your jacket."

He kissed down her belly as he remembered that moment. "Halloween?" He pressed harder with his fingers.

"Yesss."

"The night you used a vibrator? Not a pencil sharpener?"

"Yes."

Moving his fingers underneath the lace, he circled her clit and she pushed up against his hand.

"Were you thinking about me when you used it?"

"Nick—"

"Did you imagine my fingers doing this to you?"

"Damn it, Detective. Why are you torturing me?"

"Oh, babe, you think that was torture?"

Pulling at the edge of her panties, he peeled them off and spread her legs. Then he swept his tongue over her wet slit, circling her clit before bringing the nub to his lips and sucking.

"Holy shit!" She bucked hard.

"That's it, babe. Let yourself go."

He sucked harder while his fingers found her nipples and pinched. Then when he felt her body tensing, he pulled away. "Damn, you taste so good. I knew you would."

"Please don't stop."

He chuckled, asking, "You liked that?" And slowly, he circled her nub with his thumb, teasing her more.

"Please, Nick!"

Leaning forward, he continued to lick and suck as he thrust one, then two fingers inside her. Damn, she was tight. Curling them, he continued his onslaught until she screamed his name, "Nick! Oh God, I'm coming!"

He didn't let up as he felt her release. And when her body relaxed, he moved up over her and stared into her eyes.

God, she was so beautiful laid out before him. How the hell could she not have had an orgasm with a man? That thought had been burning a hole in his brain since she told him. Now that he knew firsthand how responsive she really was, it confirmed to him that she must have dated some real losers in the past. He planned to make up for all those lost orgasms if she'd let him.

She reached out and cupped his cheek. "That was incredible. I don't understand how you did that. And so fast."

"That was me just getting started," he assured her as a satisfied smile sat on her lips.

"Now can you please take off your pants?"

"You can't wait to see the goods, can you?"

She laughed.

Standing, he pulled down his zipper and yanked off his jeans and his boxer briefs. A swell of pride came over him when he saw her eyes widen. "You like?"

Her lips curved into a smile. "I already knew you had the goods to back up that arrogant attitude of yours."

Reaching down, he grabbed a foil packet from his pants. "I thought I caught you staring at my crotch a few times."

"No, it was when you came out of your room the morning William's boxes arrived. Trust me, the last thing I wanted to deal with at that moment was someone at the door." With that, she sat up and grasped his arms, pulling him down onto the bed. Then while she watched him with an expression full of anticipation, he stroked himself a few times before rolling on the condom.

"Are you ready?" He rubbed her clit with the head of his cock as he waited for her confirmation.

She answered by grabbing his ass and pulling him in. She was so tight and warm and perfect, he couldn't control himself, and he was fully seated in seconds. "You feel so damn good."

Her legs squeezed around his waist and she urged him to move. He tried to maintain control as he thrust in and out. "I want to fuck you so hard," he ground out.

"So do it." Her hand slapped his ass, catching him off guard, and when he drove into her harder, she raked her nails down his spine, which nearly sent him over the edge.

"Get on your back, soldier," she told him, and he was happy to oblige.

He flipped over, taking her with him, and the sight of her grinding against him as she rode him hard was the sexiest thing he'd ever seen. Then she swiveled her hips, and he just about came undone.

"I'm not going to last. I need you to come for me again, all right?"

A frown flashed across her mouth and

darkness crossed her eyes. He was going to wipe that doubt off her face, even if they had to keep having sex to do it. He grinned at the thought, then his fingers found her clit and he rubbed until he felt her squeezing him.

"Oh! Oh!" She climaxed, and he lost all control, picking up the pace and thrusting up into her until he found his own release.

She fell onto his chest, lying there until they caught their breath. Then she rolled to his side, and he took that moment to dispose of the condom. When he returned, she was getting dressed.

"What are you doing?"

"I thought I should go to my room. Well, if I can walk. My legs are like jelly—"

He picked her up and put her back on the bed, then he crawled up and pulled her into his arms.

"That was very caveman of you," Lauren said as she cuddled into his chest.

He grunted. He needed a moment before he spoke because the words that were on his lips were not what he was willing to say yet.

That had been, hands down, the best sex of his life and there was no way he could go without her in his arms tonight.

"Stay." Was all he could manage.

She pushed herself up on an elbow. "In your room? All night?"

"Yes."

Her eyes searched his. He had no idea what she must see, but she smiled. "Sure." Then she settled back into his arms.

"I can't believe you were able to make me orgasm. I thought I had faulty equipment."

"Twice. I made you orgasm twice. And your equipment is perfect. The next time I see Scott, I should punch him for not treating you right."

Her arms tightened around him, and damn if that didn't feel right.

"Thank you."

Two words that made his heart flip. That's when he knew. He'd fallen for her.

★ ★ ★

Lauren woke a few hours later with the strong need to go pee. She pried herself out of Nick's arms and ran to the bathroom.

Holy shit. That had been the hottest sex of her life. When she washed her hands, she caught herself smiling in the mirror. This was one night she'd never forget. And now, all she wanted was a repeat.

She climbed back into bed and Nick pulled her to him.

"You awake?"

"No, just sleep cuddling," he said.

Cuddling with this man felt so right. But it also

scared her. She was getting way too attached and she had no idea where her future would be. Staying in Fisher Springs was supposed to be a temporary move until she could afford a place somewhere else. Anywhere she could get a position in accounting. Losing her last job had gutted her. She'd loved that job. But the grief from her mom's death had been too strong. She couldn't concentrate. She wasn't shocked when they let her go.

Then when she came to Fisher Springs, she was surprised there wasn't one opening for an accountant.

Any city would do. Maybe Nick would follow her. Or would he stay here? He wasn't really putting down any roots in the town. She had no idea what his plans were.

"Nick?"

"Hmm?"

"Why did you come to Fisher Springs?"

"For a job."

"I know, but why apply here? Did you visit once and love it so much you want to retire here?"

Oh no. She squeezed her eyes shut. He was going to see through that and think she already had their wedding and kids figured out.

His arms tightened around her.

"I was strongly advised to leave my last job for a while. I screwed up on a case. Fisher Springs had an opening and it wasn't too far from my family. I applied and here I am for a while."

"For a while? You plan to go back?"

"I did. Now I'm not sure. But even if I did, it isn't that far from here, you know."

"Oh, okay. I was just curious."

"What about you? Do you plan to leave the area?" His palm moved along her skin and his touch had her revved up in no time.

"I might have to. Before I came here, I was an accountant and there are no accounting jobs here." She kissed his neck as her hands roamed over his chest. She admired how muscular he was, and she had appreciated those strong arms around her last night.

"There are no accounting jobs?" he asked.

"Yep. Not surprising. It is a small town."

"Huh. I bet something will open up."

"Maybe." She continued to run her hands over his body. "You were in the Army?"

"Yep."

"How long?"

"Four years. I signed up after high school but then decided not to reenlist. I joined the police academy instead."

She propped herself up on her elbow. "You didn't go to college?"

His body tensed. "No. Is that a problem?"

"Of course not," she said as she kissed his jaw. "But after seeing where you're from, I suspect your parents wanted you to."

"They did. They're very disappointed in my choices."

"I'm sorry. That can't be easy to live with."

Before she knew what had happened, Nick had her on her back and was between her legs, looking her directly in the eye.

"I can't keep talking with your hands all over me like that."

"Okay. No more talking," she said.

Then he was kissing her within an inch of her life while pressing something very hard against her slit. All she could do was moan as she moved her hips to get closer to him.

"Now it's time to show you how a man properly makes love to a woman."

Makes love?

Before she could dwell on that, he had her distracted with those talented fingers of his.

Chapter Twenty

After an incredible weekend with Lauren, Nick's bubble burst when he heard Grace come in the front door.

"Hello! Anyone home?"

Lauren grumbled in his arms.

"Guess we better get up and get dressed," Nick told her.

Her grip tightened around him. "No, I want to stay here all day."

He kissed the top of her head. "Me too, but Grace will soon find us. Besides, I have to work today."

She sat up. "Seriously?"

He stood and pulled on his pants. "Yep. Lots of crime on Sunday in this town." He flashed her a grin. As if on cue, his cell phone buzzed on the nightstand. He swiped open the message then groaned.

"Anyone else get ransacked?"

"No. But Ms. Finkle's cat got stuck in the crawl space again."

He pulled off his pants and traded them for jeans.

Lauren tossed on her sweater then laughed. "Since when do detectives get called for lost cats?"

"Don't get me started." He buttoned up his shirt, then went to the bathroom and quickly brushed his teeth.

"Go ahead, I want to know." She was dressed and, in the doorway, wearing a grin.

"I didn't know Ms. Finkle lost her cat every five minutes. One night when I was at the station alone, she called in. I had nothing else to do, so I helped her out. Now, almost daily, she calls me to help find her cat."

Lauren laughed. "Well, why not ask Harvey to go?"

He closed his eyes. "Apparently, the chief has a no-lost-cat-calls rule that I didn't know about. Neither he nor Harvey will respond. Plus, I gave Ms. Finkle my cell number."

Lauren fell onto the bed laughing. "I'm sorry. You probably don't find this funny, but it is."

"It's all right. I've had worse calls. As the new guy in town, I get the calls the others don't want to take."

"I'd love to hear about those sometime."

A creak on the stairs caught his attention.

"There you two are." Grace beamed. She walked in the room and took in the unmade bed and their bed heads and her smile fell.

"Yes, here we are," said Lauren, a fake smile plastered on her face.

"Okay, well, I didn't mean to intrude. I was simply curious if anyone was here."

"Grace, you're not intruding. I was about to leave. I'll see you later, Lauren." Nick gave Lauren a kiss then grabbed his keys and left. With any luck, it would be a light day and he'd be back in bed with her soon.

★ ★ ★

Nick returned to the mansion after dark. So much for an easy day. After he rescued the Finkle cat, he got called up to the town hall, where two out-of-towners had reported a dead body. Turns out, it was part of a Halloween decoration no one packed away. A running joke to the locals. Not so funny to the out-of-towners.

Then he'd almost made it back to the mansion when a theft call came in. The big theft turned out to be that several ornaments were missing off a resident's newly decorated outdoor tree. It wouldn't have been so bad except the call also went to the county sheriff, who sent in a car. Of course, he knew the guys. While they stood there staring at the tree in question, a squirrel ran up, grabbed a small ornament, and took off with it.

The deputies thought it was the funniest thing. "You got a lot of major crime here, don't you, Moore?"

He'd flipped them the bird, and now, here he was. He should probably start looking for an apartment. He'd agreed to stay at the mansion for a few days and next thing he knew, it'd been a month. That's what happens when you don't solve who ransacked the house. That bothered him. There was no DNA on anything he collected. While he suspected William was involved, no further incidences had occurred, but then, everyone knew he was staying there. And that was why he couldn't leave, because what might happen if he left? Even though it would be best to find his own place in order to give him and Lauren some space as they explored this new relationship.

Relationship. He never thought he'd say those words again.

His phone vibrated. Looks like his old coworker Dillon had dug deeper and had sent him William's credit report. He tapped it open and as he read, his stomach churned. William was supposed to be rich, yet according to the report, his credit cards were maxed out and he'd had a mortgage go into foreclosure. This didn't make sense. There had to be a mix-up. He called his friend.

"Hey, Nick," Dillon answered. "I'm guessing you saw the report?"

"Yeah, it can't be right."

"That's what I thought, but I verified it. Two of those maxed-out credit cards are technically business cards that are in his name. I have to say I'm surprised. I really thought this guy was the one funding Carl's operation down there."

This meant William was mixed up with Carl but not funding him. That didn't bode well.

"The man's broke?"

"Yep."

"And no arrest record?"

"None."

Nick scrubbed his hand along his jaw. "Well, that might explain why he's staying here then."

"Be careful. We have no idea what this guy's into, but Carl isn't someone you want to be associated with. You still calling the Oregon officer tomorrow?"

"Yeah."

"Let me know what you find out."

"Will do. Thank you." Nick pocketed the phone.

Well, well, William. What are you hiding?

He pushed that out of his mind for now. There was nothing he could do about it tonight, and besides, he couldn't help but smile as he looked forward to a quiet evening in with Lauren. Once he got to the mansion, however, the smile fell off his face when he walked inside and heard William's voice coming from the kitchen. As he got closer, Nick saw that he and Grace were sitting with Lauren at the table.

"Nick!" Lauren jumped up and pulled him in for a hug.

Wasn't hard to miss the sneer on William's face. Nick flashed him a grin and wrapped his arms around his girl.

"Nick, you're just in time for happy hour. Here, I'll mix up something for you." Grace was already up and starting to pour. "We should all thank William. My drinks wouldn't taste so good if it weren't for his present."

Grace held up a nice bottle of whiskey.

"I thought top shelf was for sipping, not mixing."

"It is," William snapped. "But Grace likes to mix drinks."

Grace brought the drink over and handed it to Nick.

"Grace, thank you, but no thank you. I'm not a hard liquor guy. I'll grab a beer." He took a bottle from the fridge and turned to see Grace offering another glass to William.

"William, you didn't have one last time. Want one now?"

"No, I'll stick to my scotch."

"How did the cat rescue go?" Lauren grinned from above her drink.

"It went fine. Other things came up."

"Huh." William grunted. "You save cats?" Then he asked Lauren, "You'd prefer that to a man who successfully took over his family's business?" He finished his scotch.

"Scott didn't take over his family's business. Not yet," Grace said.

William smiled, but it didn't reach his eyes, which swept over Lauren's body. "Yeah, Scott."

Nick had to shut this guy down now. But when he stepped in front of Lauren, the prick chuckled.

"I'd hardly say Scott was a catch," Grace said.

William turned to face Grace. "Better than a small-town cop." He made his way to the bar and poured himself another drink. "I'll be in my room."

After William left, Nick fell into his seat.

"The nerve of that guy." Nick took a pull of his beer; glad William had left the room but still not happy he was in the same house as Lauren. The last thing Lauren needed was someone staring at her like she was a piece of meat. Perhaps his plans for finding an apartment should wait until after the holidays.

"Please excuse him. He's grieving. He was very close to his father."

Lauren set her drink down. "He was? I never

saw them together."

Grace cocked her head. "Well, yes, they worked together at Chanler Enterprises."

"I thought he worked in the Portland office," Nick said.

"Yes, he does now. But for years he worked side by side with his father in the office here. They'd drive in together every morning."

"You call him hitting on his stepsister grieving?" Nick's grip on his beer tightened. He couldn't wait to call the Portland officer in the morning. Best case would be to find out William was a wanted man and he could arrest him. Unlikely, but he'd fantasized about cuffing William and taking him in.

"What are you talking about? He didn't hit on Lauren. He was pushing for Scott. Not that he should have been."

Nick opened his mouth to fill her in on William, but then another question struck him. "Why would William push Scott on Lauren? Why would he care?"

Nick watched as Grace's face lit up.

There was no doubt about it. Grace liked to gossip. Or maybe she wanted to be the center of attention. Or maybe it was the drinks. Although the drink in front of her appeared untouched.

"William's best friend in high school was Scott's cousin. I think he's always liked Scott, despite their age difference."

"I still don't like William," Nick told her.

"Grief makes people behave in strange ways. The William I've seen this last month is not the William I know. Please give him time. He'll return to his old self." Grace patted Nick's arm and stood up.

"Hmm. And what if what you're seeing now *is* the real William?" Nick asked.

"I've known him since he was a boy. It's not."

Before Nick could press further, Lauren intervened. "Grace, these drinks really are good. What's in them again?" Lauren's hand squeezed Nick's leg under the table. He got the message. Back off.

"Oh yes, this is an old recipe my grandma used to make. Then my mom made it for my dad when he'd get home from work. I always thought I'd do the same. I'll have to write it down for you so you can make it for Nick sometime."

"Well, maybe just for me. I'd love another."

"You can have the one I made for Nick if you'd like."

"Maybe you can take that drink to go." Nick nodded upstairs in case she didn't get the hint.

"Oh, no worries. I was about to head off to bed," Grace said as she slid the drink in front of Lauren.

"Good night, you two." Grace turned to leave.

"Good night, Grace!" Lauren called out.

"This really is good."

Nick reached for it to take a sip. He was curious what exactly Lauren liked. As soon as he did, he wished he hadn't.

"It's bitter. You like this?"

Lauren laughed. "It has a lot of lemon in it. But once you get past that, it gets sweet."

Nick wasn't so sure about that. But then he wasn't exactly a foodie so what did he know?

"Is this happy hour a daily tradition?" he asked.

Lauren took a long sip. "Seems to be, doesn't it? Maybe it's a holiday thing."

"Speaking of holidays, I saw they're doing the town tree lighting next Saturday. Want to go?" he asked.

She grinned. "Yeah, I do."

"Want to go upstairs now?" He leaned in and kissed her.

"Yeah, I do."

Chapter Twenty-One

The moment Lauren woke up, she was out of bed and running to the bathroom. She was nauseated, terribly thirsty, and then started vomiting.

"Lauren." Nick knelt by her side, pulling her hair back.

After she'd finished, she sat against the wall. "You better keep your distance. Looks like I have the flu."

"Do you think you're going to vomit again?"

She shook her head. Actually, she already felt a little better.

"I'll be right back. I'm going to get you some water."

Nick left and she closed her eyes. Working at the diner put her right out there with all sorts of viruses. She'd likely be sick throughout the entire winter.

"Lauren? Are you all right?"

Her eyes popped open and Grace was there.

"I'm a little nauseated."

Grace smiled. "Oh, honey!"

"Why are you smiling?"

"Well, isn't it obvious?"

Another wave of nausea was coming on. "No."

"You're pregnant!"

Fear gripped her. No, she couldn't be. Or if she was, this was way too soon to have morning sickness. But she couldn't tell her aunt that. Everyone thought she and Nick had been hot and heavy for well over a month.

Nick returned with a mug of water and a box of crackers.

"Here's some water. I brought crackers for when you feel a little better."

"Nick, you need to go to the store and buy a pregnancy test right now," Grace commanded.

His jaw dropped. "What?"

He knelt by Lauren again, concern shining in his eyes. The emotion pouring from him was overwhelming. "You're pregnant?"

"No."

"I'm sure she is," Grace said.

Lauren shook her head.

"I'm going to run to the store and get a test. Do you need anything else?" Nick asked.

She shook her head again, fearing that if she spoke, the tears would start.

"Okay, I'll be back soon." He kissed her lightly, then left.

She didn't want him to leave, but she couldn't discuss this in front of Grace. When her stomach constricted again, she groaned.

"I'll make you some ginger tea. Perfect for nausea and safe for pregnancy," Grace beamed.

"I'm not pregnant. It's just the flu." If she said it enough, maybe Grace would listen.

"We'll see," Grace singsonged as she left.

Lauren stayed by the toilet in case she got sick again, and a few minutes later, Grace returned, carrying a steaming mug. "Here you are. Drink this and you'll feel better."

Lauren frowned. "It smells."

"Don't worry. It's only ginger."

She had nothing to lose at this point and needed to get to work. Lauren drank down the tea and ate the crackers Nick brought her. Gradually, she began to feel like herself again.

Nick returned with a white plastic bag. He reached into it and pulled out a pregnancy test.

"I'll give you two some privacy." Grace left the room.

Nick sat on the edge of her bed. "Whatever it says, I'm here for you."

"Nick, there's no way I'm pregnant. We've

only been having sex for less than a week. But we can't tell Grace that."

"Oh. Right. Well, take the test anyway so you can show Grace. I'll wait out here."

After peeing on a stick, she called out, "Nick?"

"Yeah, I'm right here." He was outside the door.

"Can you set a timer for three minutes?"

"Sure."

Leaving the test on the counter, she fell back against the wall and slid to the floor. The nausea had passed. She'd have to remember to thank Grace for her tea.

A beeping sound came from the hallway.

"Three minutes is up. Can I come in?"

She crawled to the door and pulled herself up. Taking a deep breath, she opened the door.

"Ready to look?"

She nodded.

The test had only one line.

"One line? What does that mean?" Nick asked.

"Not pregnant."

She couldn't read his expression. "What are you thinking?"

"I thought for a moment you could be pregnant with Scott's baby, and everything about that seemed wrong."

"That wouldn't have been possible."

His head whipped up. "Why not?"

"We hadn't been together for months before we broke up and that was months ago. If I'd been pregnant by him, I'd be as big as a house."

"I've never done that before. You know, waited on a pregnancy test."

"Well, I'm happy to be your first."

He arched a brow.

"A little humor. I kind of need it right now," she said.

He put his arms around her, and they stood there for a moment. Then she shoved him away.

"What's wrong?"

"Well, if I'm not pregnant, I might have the flu. You need to stay back."

He stood there, staring at her.

"What is it?" she asked.

"I have to go to work. I don't want to leave you here alone."

"Go. It's okay. I'm starting to feel a little better."

★ ★ ★

Two hours later, Lauren was in full swing at the restaurant. She was still a bit under the weather but so much better than earlier. It must have been food poisoning, although she wasn't sure from what.

Her mind kept going to the pregnancy test. There was no way she was ready for kids, but she did want them someday. Once she was married, she'd love them. She could picture little Nicks running around.

She froze. *Little Nicks?* Then a smile crossed her face. Yep, little Nicks.

"Miss? Is everything all right?"

She snapped back to reality and six heads at the table were looking at her. She'd spaced out while taking an order. She'd never done anything like that before.

"I'm sorry. I didn't get enough sleep last night." Not bad for a cover. "Let's go over your order again."

Once that fiasco was resolved, she took a deep breath and admired all the decorations.

Everything about the diner put her in a better mood. Christmas music played over the speakers, Harmony and their boss had hung lit garland all around the window and a few fake wreaths on the walls, and there was even a small Christmas tree in the corner, decorated with red ornaments and lights and a stuffed llama that was squeezed in amongst the branches. She had to laugh. Harmony knew of her obsession with llamas, and she was certain that was there for her.

The diner smelled of Christmas too. Harmony had insisted they keep a cinnamon candle going so the entire placed carried the scent of baked goods. All they needed now was for it to snow and it would be picture perfect. Well, almost. Nothing would be perfect with her mother gone. She'd done a great job of keeping her mind occupied, but the holidays always reminded her of the ones she had growing up. She quelled down the anger when she thought of how many she'd missed since her mom married Michael.

"I love how you all decorated this place. This is my favorite time of year." Ms. Finkle was standing beside Lauren.

"This is the first time I've been here for the holidays. I'd say it's probably my favorite time of year here too." Lauren grinned down at the older woman who met at the diner with three other women once a week for coffee and pie.

"The holidays make you realize what all we should be thankful for, don't you think?" Ms. Finkle smiled up at her.

Lauren's mind went straight to Nick. She was thankful he'd entered her life. She'd managed to push most people away, and while she might not have originally appreciated his smug attitude, it turns out, he was quite protective, and she found that incredibly attractive. Well, that and his well-toned body.

"Yes, they do," she said while imagining what she wanted to do to Nick later.

"I'm glad we're on the same page. There's someone here I think you should give another chance."

Another chance?

Lauren's gaze snapped toward the older

woman, but she was no longer at her side. Instead, everyone was staring out the front window, where a man stood in front of the bright headlights of a car. The extra cloud cover this time of year caused it to be darker than normal. When she moved closer to get a better view, her breath caught. "Oh no."

Scott was standing in front of his car, holding white poster size cards. When his eyes caught Lauren's, he flipped one of them around. In large black letters, it read "I am nothing without you."

"Ah, would you look at that! He's recreating that scene from that movie. How romantic!" someone behind her said.

Then he tossed the card down and held up the next one. "I will love you until the end of time."

Lauren closed her eyes. All those years, and Scott had never done anything romantic. Now this. She knew his real purpose. A show. He was putting on a show for the town and they were eating it up.

"Lauren, go put that boy out of his misery." Ms. Finkle was at her side again.

When she opened her eyes, Scott was holding a new card. "Please give me another chance." Then he stood there, his face full of love and hope.

"I can't believe he'd take her back after she cheated on him." The voice came from behind her. That was the last straw. She swiveled on her heel.

"I did not cheat on him," she said loud enough for everyone to hear. "He cheated on *me* with his assistant. I walked in on them together."

Several people gasped.

"What was he supposed to do after you went off with the detective?" She turned to see Marjorie standing there, hands on her hips. Marjorie was Scott's ex from high school. She'd always believed she was meant for Scott, and she hated Lauren.

"You've always wanted him back, Marjorie. Here's your chance."

Ignoring the collective gasp, Lauren stormed to the break room before she said anything more she'd regret. The town loved Marjorie and she was certain she'd catch hell for her tongue-lashing tomorrow. But she'd deal with that then.

"Oh, honey, I'm so sorry he did this to you." Harmony was by her side.

Lauren's hands were trembling. The nausea from earlier returned.

"I need to leave."

Harmony nodded. "Go ahead. I got this covered."

"Thank you." Lauren hugged her friend, then left out the back door.

By the time she parked in front of the mansion, she was feeling better. Nick's car wasn't there, so she sent him a quick text asking when he'd be home. Then she braced herself for possibly seeing William. Merely the sight of him put her in a foul mood.

Her phone dinged.

"I'll be late. A man is stuck in a chimney and claims it's Santa's fault. Wants to press charges…"

She chuckled then texted, "Welcome to Fisher Springs."

His reply came fast. "Yeah…there's something in the water here…"

She tossed her phone in her purse and took a deep breath. Maybe she could sneak upstairs and get a nap in before Nick got back.

Once she stepped inside, her senses were hit with a savory smell. Her stomach growled. With her nausea at bay for the moment, she walked into the kitchen. Grace was stirring something in a large pot.

"Lauren! I'm glad you're home. I made a stew."

Maybe this wouldn't be so bad after all. "Wow, that smells fantastic." Her stomach grumbled, reminding her that she hadn't been up to eating lunch.

"It'll be ready in about twenty minutes. I was about to get our happy hour drinks."

Lauren went into the kitchen and spotted William hunched over the table, reading something on his phone.

"Happy hour? Again? I shouldn't. I've been feeling on and off fluish."

Grace frowned. "I'm sorry, dear. But you know, back in my mom's day, they would drink whiskey to chase off the flu."

Lauren glanced at William, who was no longer

focused on his phone. He was frowning at Grace's comment.

"I think you mean whiskey for a cold," William said.

"Colds, flu, just about anything. Anyway, I'll add some ginger to the drink. I was able to grow some ginger root in my greenhouse. Isn't that amazing?"

Lauren shrugged. "Well, it has been pretty warm for this time of year." She took a seat at the table opposite William.

"Your greenhouse?" William asked. "I thought you didn't use it in the winter."

"Well it's not winter yet, is it?" Grace hummed as she mixed the drinks. Then she set them on the table and sat down.

"Are you ready to try one, William?"

He gave her a rare smile. "Sure. Why not." Grace handed a glass to William.

"Mmm. This is good," he said.

Grace grasped Lauren and William's hands.

"I'm so happy you two are here. After Michael and Candy passed, I'm afraid I wasn't sure I had any family left. This last month has been great." Grace released their hands and reached for her drink. "A toast to family."

They all clinked glasses and took a sip.

"Speaking of a month," William turned to Lauren, "How long do you plan to stay here?

"William, don't be rude," Grace said, then took

a drink. "Lauren can stay here as long as she wants."

"No, it's all right. I don't mean to overstay. I'm trying to save up enough to get an apartment." Lauren took several large gulps.

Maybe if she finished her drink, she could excuse herself.

A smile spread over William's face. "Well, Lauren, if you'd like, I can front you the money. I know you and Nick must want your privacy. Also, why is he still here again?" He leaned forward, staring at her.

"Nick's here because someone broke in and they haven't caught the person yet."

William leaned back and clasped his hands. "That was a month ago. I asked around and it turns out, he was staying in a motel for a few days before he moved in here."

"So?" Lauren drank down more of her drink.

"So, he doesn't have anywhere to live and seems to be enjoying staying here for free. I don't like it. From what I hear in town, no one much cares for him. Oh, I meant to ask, did Scott find you?"

What the hell? She'd had enough of this at the restaurant. She wasn't going to tolerate it here too. "Scott?"

"Yeah, he came by with flowers. They're over there." He pointed and nearly spilled his drink.

"You told him where I was?"

"I said you were at work. He's a decent guy,

you know. You should give him a chance."

"Oh no, not again. I'm not getting back together with Scott. And the town has an issue with Nick because of rumors Scott spread. Nick's a good guy. But I get the message loud and clear—we're not welcome. We'll move out this weekend."

After tossing the last sip down, she slammed her glass on the table and stormed off.

"Lauren, come back! You forgot to eat some stew!" Grace yelled after her.

Damn you, William. She couldn't stand to be in the same room with him another minute. Moving would be the best choice. Once she was out of this house, she'd have no more reason to ever see William again. They weren't really even family. But a pang of sadness hit when she thought about Grace. She'd miss her. Her aunt was like a second mother to her. For years, it had been only her and her mom. Now that Grace was in her life, she didn't want to give that up. Living in the same town, she hoped she wouldn't have to.

All of a sudden, the nausea hit hard again. Then her stomach cramped. She was going to vomit. Quickly, she ran to the bathroom.

After what felt like hours of vomiting, she curled up on the cold tile floor and closed her eyes.

Chapter Twenty-Two

Red was all Nick could see when he heard about Scott's stunt. It turned out, the chimney call he went out to was bogus and timed right when Scott was trying to woo his woman.

His woman. He liked how that sounded. Hopefully, she still was his. Damn Harvey. He knew he was behind it. He was on his way to the station to give Harvey a piece of his mind when a real call came in.

By the time Nick had made it back to the station a couple of hours later, Harvey was happy to fill him in on what he'd missed. Harvey made a point to leave off Lauren's reaction and Nick sure as hell wasn't going to give him the satisfaction of asking about it.

Nope. He reported in with the police chief and

left.

On his drive back to the mansion, his phone rang.

"Nick," he answered. Thank goodness for Bluetooth.

"Nick Moore? This is detective Nolan from Portland. One of our informants gave us some new information about William Chanler. It doesn't help our case, but it might help you."

"Hope it does."

"According to the guy, William owes their boss six figures."

"And he ran."

"Yep, he ran."

"Was it for drugs?" William didn't seem like he was on drugs, but nothing would surprise Nick at this point.

"Gambling. Anyway, if these guys find him, well, it won't end well."

"Thanks for letting me know."

"Anytime." The detective ended the call.

Okay, now he had a motive. William probably needed to sell the house. But why not just explain he needed the money and sell it?

The road to the mansion stretched on longer today than usual, but he finally made it. Once inside the door, he ran up the stairs to Lauren's room.

Empty. Her shift should have ended hours ago. Where could she be?

His stomach fell as he imagined her with Scott. Then he heard a moan from the bathroom.

"Lauren?"

"In here," she groaned.

He opened the bathroom door and Lauren was lying on the floor, dark circles under her eyes and looking like death warmed over.

He bent down and felt her head. No fever.

"I've been vomiting for hours. I think I'm done, but I don't have the energy to move."

"I'll help you."

He reached one arm under her knees and the other around her shoulders and lifted her up.

"Why are your arms made of chocolate? I want chocolate," she said before her eyes rolled to the back of her head.

"Lauren?"

She went limp. She was out.

"Lauren?"

Nothing. How could she have gotten this sick so quickly? Her breathing was shallow.

Instead of taking her to her room, he took her to his car, laid her in the back seat, and headed to the hospital, which was in the next town.

During the drive, Lauren came to. "Where are we?"

"I'm taking you to the hospital."

Lauren sat up. "No, Nick. I'm sure it's just the flu."

"You passed out, Lauren. You also weren't making any sense. I'm not taking any chances."

He stared at her through the rearview mirror. She wrapped her arms around herself.

"What are your symptoms?"

"Dizzy, nauseated, and my stomach's upset. It's got to be the flu."

Turning into the parking lot, he grabbed a spot up near the front. Then he got out, walked around the car, and opened her door. "All right. Let's get you inside."

He helped her into the admitting area of the ER. While he was talking to the intake nurse, Lauren reached for his arm.

"I think I'm going to pass out again."

When she started to fall, he caught her.

"Let's get her on a gurney," the nurse said.

Nick laid her down and her eyes opened, then she turned her head away from him and vomited all over the floor.

"We're going to take her back immediately. You wait here. We'll let you know what's going on as soon we find out."

Lauren was wheeled through the double doors to the emergency room. Someone came within minutes and cleaned up the vomit. Nick studied the waiting area. He'd been to his fair share of emergency rooms in his career but never any in a small town. The room was larger than he'd expected and there was a television turned to some home improvement show.

The nurse returned to the front desk. "Sir? Can you come up here and fill out some paperwork?"

"How's she doing?" he asked.

"The doctor's with her now. She'll come out and talk to you soon. Here are the forms and a pen. Fill them out as best you can."

Nick took the clipboard and pen and sat down. Why had she gotten so sick? He didn't know anyone else in town with the flu. Not that that meant it couldn't hit her first.

He pored over the papers, realizing there was so much about her he didn't know. He didn't even know her middle name. After doing the best he could and turning them in, he returned and stared at the television. People were looking for a bargain lakefront house. He'd love to live in a lakefront house, but that wasn't something he could afford on his salary.

"Are you the man who brought in Ms. Harrow?" A doctor stood a few feet away.

Nick rose. "Yes."

"Go ahead and sit down." She took a seat in the chair across from him. "I'm Doctor Martin."

Nick held his hand out. "Detective Nick Moore."

She shook it. "This is a police investigation then?"

He frowned. "No, Lauren's my girlfriend." He

was surprised how easily those words fell from his lips. But they felt right. "Is it the flu?" he asked.

"Well, Ms. Harrow gave us consent to discuss her medical condition with you. It's not the flu. And I'll be honest, I'm not certain what it is. We're running a number of tests. It could be a virus. It could be food poisoning. Do you know what she's eaten recently?"

"Food poisoning?" He had no idea what she might have eaten from the diner.

"Has anyone else come in with food poisoning? She often eats at the diner she works at."

"No one else has come in with her symptoms."

His mind immediately went to William. Would he deliberately try to hurt her? He did want her out of the house. How far would he go?

"Could it be a deliberate poisoning?"

The doctor's eyebrows shot up. "I can't say with any certainty based on her general symptoms. I can run a tox screen, but that will only look for a small number of toxins. What gives you the idea that she was poisoned?"

He ran his hand through his hair. "I don't know for sure. It's a gut feeling."

"Do you know what Ms. Harrow ate or drank today?"

"No, I had just finished my shift when I found her like this. She worked at the diner earlier. Then she went home. Beyond that, I have no idea."

"I'll ask her to give us details on what she's

consumed in the last twenty-four hours."

His stomach churned. "What was her blood alcohol level?"

The doctor pursed her lips.

"I know you check the blood alcohol level of any incoming patient. What was hers?"

Doctor Martin opened the folder she was holding. "It was 0.05."

"Shit." He'd had a bad feeling about William and the way he treated Lauren from the beginning. On top of that, why didn't he drink the whiskey he brought? They had another damn happy hour tonight. But would William go so far as to poison Lauren? And why would he? No, it didn't make any sense. Unless Lauren wasn't his intended victim. It was Grace who made a big deal about happy hour and making those drinks. But William would have known the recipe.

Or was Nick the intended mark? William had made it clear he was unhappy with his presence at the mansion. He thought back to the few happy hours they'd all had together. Grace had been so excited about the whiskey William brought. But then he watched William skip over the whiskey and pour himself a Scotch. "Son of a bitch."

"Detective?"

"Her stepbrother brought a bottle of whiskey, but he never drank from it."

"And Ms. Harrow did?"

"Yes."

"And you have reason to believe it was poisoned?"

"Like I said, it's a gut feeling. I'll get the bottle tested." How the hell was he going to do that without a warrant or open case?

Doctor Martin stood. "I've got to get back to Ms. Harrow."

"Thank you," Nick said.

★ ★ ★

When she woke up, Lauren didn't recognize the white ceiling tile. Her head pounded and she reached up to wipe her eyes. The pull on her arm stopped her. Glancing down, she saw the IV hooked into her arm. A low but constant beeping sound came from behind her.

"What the—"

"Lauren?"

Her head jerked to her left, where she spotted Nick in a chair with a blanket on his legs.

"Babe, I'm happy to see those amber eyes of yours." He was at her side, holding her hand.

Despite her surroundings, her heart clenched at his endearment. "What happened?"

His gaze shifted down. He rubbed the back of her hand with his fingers. "The doctors are still trying to figure that out. I found you nearly delirious on the bathroom floor. Do you remember?"

Flipping through her memories, she recalled having a drink with Grace and William and then making an excuse to go upstairs and be alone.

"I remember Grace made us drinks and William wasn't being nice. I drank it fast and then went upstairs. Then I got sick." She turned away, groaning. "I didn't eat any dinner. And Grace made the drink stronger than normal. Alcohol on an empty stomach. Such an amateur move." She stared out the window, embarrassed she'd ended up in the hospital.

"The doctor doesn't think that's what made you sick."

Her head jerked back. "No?" She'd felt a little nauseated before the drink.

"Is it the flu? I felt nauseated when I drove home last night, but then Grace insisted whiskey would help fight it off."

He licked his lips. "Lauren, that wasn't last night. And, no, the doctor ran a number of tests. She ruled out flu."

The monitor started beeping faster. She didn't have to look to know her heart rate had sped up.

"Not last night? How long have I been here?"

"About thirty-six hours."

She squeezed her eyes shut. "I can't be here. I'm supposed to be working. I had shifts scheduled every day this week. This is their busy season with the holiday festival and ice rink."

His hand squeezed hers. "It's all right. I called and explained. It's not like you had a choice."

"If it wasn't the alcohol or flu, what's wrong with me?" She felt the tears coming but was helpless to stop them.

"The doctor suspects you were poisoned in some way, but the test results haven't come back yet."

"Poisoned? How?"

"No one knows anything for certain yet. It could be food poisoning."

A nurse came into the room.

"Ms. Harrow, I'm happy you're awake."

A woman walked in behind the nurse, holding a chart. "Ms. Harrow, I'm Doctor Martin. It's good to see that you're alert."

"Doctor, have the tests come back?" Nick asked.

Doctor Martin set the chart down on the table. "I'm afraid these tests take longer to run. For now, based upon her symptoms and what the blood tests have ruled out, we've been treating this as a poisoning."

The doctor turned to Lauren. "Do you recall eating or drinking anything that tasted bitter or off?"

Bitter? Her food had been rather bland. But the happy hour drinks had been bitter. No! She looked at Nick. "The happy hour drinks."

He nodded.

"Every day for the past week, my aunt has been making drinks for us. She said it was a family recipe. It was a bit bitter. Then I felt sick, but it got better."

"If you can keep lunch down, I'll put in the orders to release you this afternoon. Whatever you do, don't drink any more of those drinks."

The doctor addressed Nick, "Detective, there isn't enough evidence here for me to submit a formal complaint with the police, but if the tox screen results come back positive, I'm required to file a police report."

"Of course," Nick replied.

Once the doctor left, Lauren's brain swam with confusion. She wanted to wish it all away. "It doesn't make sense, Nick. Grace is like a mom to me. What would she possibly have to gain by poisoning me and William?"

"It might not be Grace. William supplied the whiskey, but he never drank it."

Her eyes widened as she thought about William. "He always drank scotch, but no, not last night. I mean, the other night. He had one of Grace's drinks."

"Are you sure?"

Her mind was fuzzy. Had he had it or did he turn it away? Why couldn't she remember?

"No, I can't be certain."

"The whiskey is at the lab being tested."

"But that doesn't make sense either. What would he gain?"

"There's something you should know." Nick stood and paced the room. "I ran a background check on William. He's not what everyone thinks he is."

"Well, I think he's an asshole CEO. That's not right?"

"He is that, but there's more. He's not rich like he wants everyone to believe. His credit cards are maxed out and his house was foreclosed upon."

Lauren sat up. "Wait, the house he offered me to live in?"

"Yes. And he's been associated with a known criminal in the Portland area."

"What kind of criminal?"

"The kind that loans money to desperate people."

"You think William owes money to a what? A loan shark? The mafia?"

Nick chuckled. "Watch TV much?"

Heat crept up her neck. "Well, not all of us are well versed in criminal terminology," she shot back.

"Fair enough. I spoke to an officer in Portland and William's been on their radar for some time. There's no proof yet, but they're convinced he's tied into some crime circles down there."

"How could that be? Michael Chanler was loaded, William should have been able to pay everything off with his inheritance."

"Well, maybe Michael wasn't as rich as you thought."

"What do you mean? He and my mom took trips all the time. And look at that mansion."

Nick furrowed his brow. "You're right. The mansion. Why wouldn't William sell it if he needed money?"

Then she remembered a conversation she had with her mother. "Because he doesn't own it. I remember my mom making sure it was in the prenup that she could live there if Michael died first. Maybe the house belonged to Michael and Grace."

"Does Grace have any children?"

She shook her head. "No, she said I was the daughter she never had."

"Well, now we have our motive. If Grace dies, her share of the house likely goes to William."

Chapter Twenty-Three
William

The doorbell was ringing nonstop. Why the hell wasn't anyone answering it? William's phone buzzed with a message.

"I'm at your front door. We need to talk."

William groaned. He'd been lying down, hoping he'd feel better. After the phone call last week, he'd been hiding out in the mansion. The stress of it was starting to get to him. Plus, he was out of his blood pressure medication. Damn, he didn't feel old enough to need daily medication. He could thank dear old dad for handing that down to him.

Dad. He'd died of a heart attack. God, he needed to go to the gym. Once upon a time, he'd cared about how he looked. That was before he got caught up in his current mess. Before he'd had to spend all his time running Chanler Enterprises.

The doorbell persisted. He kicked his stew bowl as he made his way out of his room. It flipped over, likely leaving a stain on the carpet. He made his way downstairs, calling out for Grace along the way. No one answered. Thank God, he was here alone. Rarely did he ever get this place to himself.

His heart was pounding in his chest as he approached the door. He took several calming breaths, then threw it open to find Scott standing there, grinning like a fool. Damn, that was definitely not going to help his blood pressure.

"What the hell are you grinning about?"

"It's good to see you too, William. You're just the person I was hoping to see. I need an advance on that payment you promised me."

The pressure in his head built and William had to remind himself to keep taking calming breaths. This idiot hadn't done a damn thing right, but he certainly wasn't going to let him raise his blood pressure. That was high enough due to other matters.

"An advance? You're shitting me, right?" William walked away from the door and toward the kitchen. At the bar, he glanced over his shoulder and Scott strutted in. The man actually strutted. William ground his teeth. He hated men like that—men who thought so highly of themselves that they would strut in and present themselves like they were being served upon a Goddamn silver platter. Nick was like that. He'd strut in and expect Lauren to melt at his feet. It wouldn't be so bad except Lauren had fallen for both of these idiots. But that wasn't what was important now.

"Nope, not shitting you, Will. I've got a hot date tonight and I need some cash."

William poured his scotch into a tumbler and then tossed it back. It burned a little more than usual going down. He was certain he could blame Scott for that. Who the hell was this guy and why did he think this would help win Lauren back?

His fingers curled tight around the counter and he glanced over his shoulder. "You mean you're hiring a date and need cash to pay her?"

When Scott acted as if he was taken aback, William spun around to face him. Scott wore an exaggerated expression of hurt. "You wound me. I don't need to buy a date."

William slammed the glass down on the counter. Amazed he didn't break it, he advised Scott, "What you need is to not date at all. You're supposed to be wooing Lauren, remember?"

Scott grinned. "I'm meeting my date outside of town. Besides, don't worry about Lauren. I'll get her back."

William poured another drink. To hell with it, he wasn't going anywhere tonight. He made it a double. "Is that right? Because so far, all I've seen is you doing a piss poor job and driving her further into the detective's arms."

Scott's jaw dropped. "What do you mean by that?"

Was this guy serious? "It's a small town. I know you've heard Lauren's been shacking up with the detective here in the mansion."

"Shacking up?" Scott's hands went to his hips.

"You know what I mean."

William drank his second shot.

"Is something wrong? I've seen you drink before, but never this fast." Scott's brow was furrowed.

"You're pissing me off. I need something to take the edge off." It was getting warm in the room, so he loosened his collar. He'd have to remember to check the thermostat.

After letting out a sigh, Scott dropped into a chair. "I'm trying everything I can, but it's not working. Most of the town is on my side. What about what you were going to do? *If* you're doing anything, it's not working."

William took a seat across from Scott and growled. "I'm also having problems with that damn detective. Everything I try, he seems to fix."

"What have you tried?"

"Loosened the railing on the porch."

Scott jumped up. "What the hell? That's not scaring Lauren out of the house—that could get her hurt."

"Well, I'm open to ideas if you have any. But if ransacking this house wasn't scary enough, I doubt you'd come up with anything better."

Damn, he was dizzy. He must have had more scotch than he realized.

Scott's eyes widened, fire blazing in them. "That was you?" Taking a step back, he crossed his arms. "When were you going to tell me that you were the one that caused this whole detective problem in the first place?"

"What the hell difference does it make? What's done is done. Besides, I have a bigger problem now."

Scott sat down again. "What's that?"

William tipped his head back and stared at the ceiling. His throat tightened and his stomach churned. What the hell was going on?

"Hey, you all right?" Scott asked.

William moved his gaze to Scott's. "What?"

"What's your bigger problem?"

He was so dehydrated. "I need something to drink." He went to the bar and poured himself a glass of water and drank it down. Then he turned to Scott.

"Lauren was taken to the emergency room a couple of days ago."

Before Scott could speak, William held up his hand. "She's fine, but the doctor says she was poisoned, and Nick's positive I did it. He came in here with a search warrant and the same as told me he thought I was guilty."

"Are you?"

"Hell no. I want her out of the house, not dead. How the hell would I get the house to myself if I'm in jail?"

A wave of nausea hit him. He clutched the counter until it passed.

Scott leaned forward and clasped his hands. "You know, I'm thinking you want more than Lauren out of this house. I mean, really, why would you pay me to take her off your hands? What's in it for you?"

"Peace and quiet. She talks too much."

Scott grinned. "You're a shitty liar. If you want peace and quiet, go back to Portland."

William winced. That would be the obvious choice to anyone who thought they knew him. But he couldn't go back to Portland. He didn't know how much longer he could really stay here before they found him. He needed to sell this house, then he could pay everyone off. But he couldn't do that with so many people coming in and out every day.

"Fucking A, Scott. I want Lauren out of this house. The why doesn't matter. Are you going to do what you promised or not?"

"Seriously, are you all right? You're pale."

"I don't feel very good. It must be the flu. Promise me you'll get her to move. She must voluntarily leave the house, or it's all been for nothing."

Scott stood and was at his side. "What are you talking about?"

The room was too hot. William unbuttoned the first several buttons. "The trust of course. The only way the house reverts back to me is if she moves out voluntarily."

He couldn't get enough air. He tried to suck in more breaths, but he couldn't.

"William, slow your breathing. You're going to pass out. Let me help you sit here on the floor."

Scott's hands were on his arms. "You're sweating. Are you having a heart attack?"

"Stomach cramps. Thirsty."

"I'm calling an ambulance." Scott helped him sag to the floor. Despite his efforts, William couldn't keep his eyes open.

"Hello, I need an ambulance. My friend is having a heart attack. Please hurry. It's the Chanler mansion. Yes, that's right."

William tried one last time to open his eyes, but when he did, he saw the darkness coming in from the corners.

"An ambulance is on the way. Hold on."

Why did he feel so sick so fast? Shit. Had he been poisoned?

"Not a heart attack," he managed to say.

"We'll let the doctors decide. Just hold on."

His eyes wouldn't open again. Everything was black.

Chapter Twenty-Four

"What did you say?" Nick couldn't believe the words he'd heard.

"William Chanler passed away this morning from a heart attack," the chief repeated.

Nick wasn't sure whether to feel relieved or more concerned. He had been certain William was the one who poisoned Lauren, but he couldn't rule out that maybe, just maybe, William had been poisoned too.

"Are you sure it was a heart attack?"

The door behind him opened and he whirled around. Grace walked in, wearing all black and carrying some sort of pie.

"Chief, this is for you. I baked a few pies last night." She then smiled up at Nick.

"Good afternoon, Nick."

Why is she smiling?

"Did you hear about William?" he asked.

She dropped her gaze. "I did, yes. So awful. I wished I'd insisted he go to the doctor the other day."

Nick glanced up at the chief, but he was too focused on the pie to pay attention to what she said.

"What happened the other day?" Nick asked.

Grace waved her hand in front of her now wet eyes.

"He hadn't been feeling well. I told him he needed to go to the doctor, get his medication changed."

"He was on medication?"

She nodded. "He had high blood pressure. Just like his father. Neither one of them took care of themselves."

Grace pulled a handkerchief from her purse. "Then he vomited the other night. I told him that was a sign of having a heart attack. He said he was fine, just had too much scotch."

She blew her nose. "And now he's gone."

"And the doctor was sure it was a heart attack?"

Grace put her hand on Nick's arm. "He had a long history with his blood pressure, and his cholesterol wasn't good. The doctor was certain."

If everyone was so certain, why was his gut twisting up over this?

"What other symptoms did he have? I should

probably know so I can keep an eye out for them. I'm not getting any younger." Nick gave her his best smile.

Her mouth dropped open.

"Nick, that's not an appropriate thing to say. The woman just lost her nephew," the chief said.

Shit, he's right. The woman was grieving and here he was probably misreading the situation.

"You're right. I'm sorry. I've got somewhere I need to be. I'll leave you two alone."

Before the chief could object, he hightailed it out of there. There was one person he needed to speak to, and it couldn't wait.

★ ★ ★

"Please close the door."

Nick closed the door and then sat in the chair across from Doctor Martin.

"What can I do for you?"

"Did you order an autopsy for William Chanler?"

The doctor leaned back in her chair. "You know I can't talk to you about a patient. Ms. Harrow asked me to talk to you about her case. This is quite different."

Nick flashed his badge. "This is part of an investigation. As you know, Lauren was poisoned—"

"Actually, we don't know that for certain. We're still awaiting test results."

He swallowed before he spoke. He'd been told he could come on too strong and alienate witnesses he was interrogating. And essentially, that's what was going on here. He needed to pull back.

"Well, it sounds like Mr. Chanler had similar symptoms with the vomiting and nausea. I'm concerned this could be a police matter."

Doctor Martin smiled. "Detective, Mr. Chanler came in with classic symptoms of a heart attack. The friend that came in with him explained everything that happened in his last moments. Mr. Chanler smoked, drank too much, and, in general, didn't take care of himself. He had high blood pressure and was stressed. There's no doubt in my mind that it was a heart attack."

"Friend? Was it a woman?" It must have been Grace.

"No, his name was Scott Fisher."

What the hell? They were friends?

"Look, I know it looks like a heart attack, but when I worked in the King County Sheriff's Office, we had a couple of poisonings that presented themselves as heart attacks. Then after the tests came back, they showed levels of a variety of poisons. I want to rule out that Mr. Chanler was a victim too."

"Isn't this the man you said poisoned Ms. Harrow?"

"Well, yes."

Her brows shot up. "And now you think *he* was poisoned? You know, Detective, sometimes a heart attack is just a heart attack."

She was smiling at him. She didn't believe any of this.

"An autopsy needs to be performed. I'll get the court order if you require that," he said through gritted teeth.

She blew out a sigh. "Actually, an autopsy won't be possible."

"Why not?"

"We released Mr. Chanler's body about an hour ago."

How the hell would she know that? He closed his eyes and tried to remember he was in a small town now.

"You released it?"

She opened the mini fridge behind her and pulled out a yogurt cup. "No, it was released by the medical examiner."

He arched a brow.

"Who's also my husband." After ripping the top off the cup, she pulled a plastic spoon from her desk drawer. "He mentioned it while we took our afternoon walk around the hospital."

"The man's body was released hours after he died?" Rubbing his scruff, he thought this through. Maybe he could get the body back for an autopsy.

"Who was it released to?"

After scooping a big spoonful of yogurt into her mouth, she set the spoon down and turned to her computer. "Let me see." She typed on the keys. "Wafford and Sons. They're located two blocks south of here."

Nick stood and rapped his knuckles on her desk. "Thank you."

He raced outside and almost ran into a group of carolers singing "We Wish You a Merry Christmas."

He smiled and then pushed past them. As he hurried down the sidewalk, he couldn't help but take in how festive everything looked. This place was decorated as much as Fisher Springs. Guess that was one nice thing about small towns. They really got into the holiday spirit.

Wafford and Sons appeared on his right and he jogged to the entrance. The door jingled when he opened it.

"Just a minute," a voice called from the back.

When he surveyed the room, he was confronted with a wall of miniature caskets, each open. It was the creepiest thing. There was also an odd smell that made him want to run out.

"Those are models so you can see the inside. Some people like to ensure that their loved ones are comfortable."

Nick spun around to see a short man in a suit

smiling at him.

"Comfortable? Are you serious?"

The man's smile dropped.

"They're dead."

The man shoved his hands in his pockets. "I take it you're not here to purchase a casket."

"No. I'm Detective Nick Moore." He pulled out his badge and held it up. "I'm here because a body was released to your custody prematurely today. It's part of an investigation and it needs to be returned to the hospital for an autopsy."

The man's eyes widened. "Oh dear. We only had one body delivered today and I'm afraid he can't be returned."

His stomach fell. "William Chanler?"

"Yes, that's the one."

"And why can't he be returned?" Nick was ready for some bureaucratic small-town crap.

"He was cremated about"—the man looked at his watch—"ten minutes ago."

That, Nick wasn't expecting. "Cremated? Who authorized that?"

"Let me pull it up. It was a nice older woman. She was quite upset, poor thing."

Grace. Damn it. Why would she do that?

"Grace Chanler. Said she was his next of kin."

Shit. "Is it normal to cremate a body so quickly after death?"

"It varies. Usually, the family takes a day or

two before they're able to come in. But Ms. Chanler was very clear. She wanted to get through the process as quickly as she could."

He squeezed his eyes shut. It was possible the woman was simply grieving. She'd lost her brother recently. But what if it was more? "The ashes. Do you have them?"

"I do."

"Can I take them?"

The man's brow furrowed. "No, I'm afraid I can't hand them over without a court order."

How the hell was he going to obtain one? The chief and doctor both believed William had a heart attack. Hell, he really didn't have any proof it wasn't a heart attack.

"Could I get a sample of the ashes?" Maybe a lab could test a small portion.

"You need to leave. Now." The man was glaring at him.

His request probably did sound off, so Nick thanked the man and headed to the door. When he left the building, the carolers were singing to a group standing on the corner across the street. He purposely bypassed them and made his way back to his car.

His phone rang. It was Dillon.

"Moore here."

"Did you talk to the officer in Portland yet?"

"I did. He had a lot to say, but none of that matters now."

"Why's that?"

"William Chanler is dead. The doctor said he died of a heart attack. Less than twelve hours after his death, his body was cremated, and there was no autopsy."

"Wow. That was fast. Do you think someone from Portland got to him?"

"No, it was Grace Chanler who authorized the cremation."

"That's weird. But didn't she just lose her brother? Sometimes people grieve in strange ways."

"Yes, if she's grieving."

"Wait, do you suspect her now?"

Nick forked his hand through his hair. "I do, but I don't have any evidence. I just have this gut feeling." Nick explained what happened to Lauren and then William.

"This sounds like the Hampton case. Do you remember that one?"

Nick closed his eyes. This sounded exactly like that case. "I do. Everyone thought the husband had a heart attack, but the daughter kept digging until she found the truth."

"Yeah, you better find out if anyone over there is a master gardener."

"I'm on it. Hey, could you look up an address for someone for me real quick?"

"Sure. Who?"

"Grace Chanler."

Chapter Twenty-Five

Lauren was happy to be out of the hospital. It had taken many hours longer than expected, but at least she was released before dinner. As Nick drove them back to the mansion, she thought of William. She couldn't believe he was dead. As much as she hated him, she'd never wished him dead.

Nick pulled up at a motel and parked.

"Why are we stopping here?"

"This is where we're staying."

She glanced at the motel and then at Nick. "Are you being serious?"

"I am."

"No, Nick. I want to go back to the mansion. All my things are there, and I want to see Grace."

A muscle in his jaw twitched as he looked at her.

"I don't think being in the mansion is such a good idea right now."

"Why would you say that? Grace is literally the only family I have left."

He let out a sigh and reached for her hand. "Remember I told you it appeared that William owed money to some bad people?"

She nodded.

"If these people come to the mansion, they aren't the type to ask questions, Lauren." He was staring out the front window as he spoke. Why wasn't he looking at her?

"Well, if that's true, we need to tell Grace so she can leave."

"I'll call her and warn her."

"I should be with her."

Nick closed his eyes. "That's not a good idea."

"Damn it, Nick. What aren't you telling me?"

"I think Grace is behind the poisoning."

She pulled her hand back as a pit formed in her stomach. Why was he saying these things?. "What? No, that doesn't make any sense. You said it was William. Then he died from a heart attack, so I'm safe. Why are you accusing Grace? What possible motive would she have to hurt me?"

"Scott was with William when he died. I spoke to him earlier and he said William's last words were 'It's not a heart attack' and his symptoms were very similar to yours. We need to see the will of Michael

Chasing Her Trust

Chanler. I believe we'll find her motive there."

"Scott? He's a liar. And why was he with William? God, he was trying to find me again, wasn't he?"

She couldn't believe this. She couldn't get rid of Scott, and now Nick was trying to control her the same way he did. First, he was trying to keep her from Grace. Then the next thing she knew, she'd be spending her nights at the motel alone while he worked late. Or what she thought was working late. No, not again.

"Take me to the mansion."

"That's not a good idea."

"It's not up to you."

He reluctantly put the car in drive and drove back to the mansion. After he parked, he turned to her. "I packed up some of your things too. We need to stay somewhere else," Nick said.

This was too much like Scott, who'd always told her what to do. She swallowed the lump in her throat as she willed tears not to fall. "You decided on your own that we would both leave the mansion?"

"It's for your safety."

For her safety?

Scott used to push her into doing things. He always said it was for her own good. Damn it. Was she destined to always fall for men who wanted to control her?

"Nick, I need space. I'm going to stay at the

mansion. Please go to the motel."

"I'm not leaving you alone in that house with that woman."

"Damn it, Nick. I will not be controlled again. Grace is a nice woman who's been nothing but a mother figure to me. She's the only one who's been there to help me through my grief. Now I'm going in there to help her through hers."

"What grief? She poisoned William!"

"Do you have proof?"

He stared back at her.

"You don't. William had health problems. It's sad he had a heart attack, but it happens all the time to people younger than him."

"I'm telling you that my gut says she did it."

"You're wrong."

He reached for her again. "Please, Lauren, come to the motel with me tonight. Tomorrow we can come here and see Grace."

"No. I need to go inside."

"Is this really about Grace?"

"What the hell does that mean?"

"I'm asking you to stay with me, but you seem hell-bent on staying at this mansion. Maybe my first impression was right."

"And what the hell was that?"

"The motel isn't anywhere as nice as this place. Money is more important to you than anything else."

Her eyes welled with tears before she could

stop them.

"I'm sorry. I didn't mean that. I'm upset—"

She cut him off before he could finish. "Go to hell, Nick. We're done." Then she yanked open the door and got out.

"Lauren, please—"

She slammed the door shut and ran up the porch steps and into the house, hoping that Nick wouldn't follow her but also almost hoping he would.

Don't look. Don't look.

She forced herself not to go back outside, and several minutes later, when she heard Nick drive away, she slid down the door until she was sitting on the ground, letting the tears fall.

"Lauren? Is that you?"

"Yes."

Grace came down the stairs. "Are you all right? Why are you on the floor?"

"I had an argument with Nick. Actually, I broke up with Nick." She wiped the tears off with her sleeve, then pulled up her knees and let her head fall to them. Getting rid of another controlling man was a good thing. But then, why did she feel so empty?

"I'm sorry. Young love. Sometimes it's easy, sometimes not so much."

"It's not love. He doesn't respect my decisions. If I don't agree with him, he says no. I can't live like that."

"Of course not, honey. It's better to know now

than after you've been married ten years."

Tears filled Lauren's eyes again as she remembered Nick's words—*Money is more important to you than anything else.* How could he say that about her? She thought he knew her. She looked up. "Grace, were you ever married?"

Grace smiled. "Yes. I'll tell you all about it while you help me." Grace held out her hand and helped Lauren up. "I'm working with some plants in the kitchen."

Lauren followed her to the kitchen and saw that the table was covered with small pots of dirt.

"What's all this?"

"Seed starters. I'm going to grow some tomatoes and lettuce."

"But it's winter."

Her aunt handed her a packet of seeds. "I have a grow light that I use during the winter months. Then when it warms up a bit, I'll transfer them to the greenhouse William got for me." Grace stilled. "My God, William. I can't believe he's gone."

Lauren hugged her aunt. "I'm sorry. I can't either."

"All of them. Gone. Too soon." Grace wiped her eyes, then took a deep breath. "You asked me a question. Yes, I was married once. He was a wonderful man."

"What happened?" Lauren asked as she opened the seed packet and looked inside.

Chasing Her Trust

Grace took it from her and poured several of them into her hand, placing one in each little cup.

"I was young. I met him at school. Todd was from the other side of town, and my father didn't approve. He didn't think he was good enough for his daughter."

"I'm sorry."

"He forbid me to see Todd. I was a good girl and I broke it off. It was hard avoiding him at school, but I tried."

Her aunt finished placing seeds in one large tray of starters.

"There. The tomatoes are done." She grabbed another seed packet with a picture of leaves on the front.

"Did Todd fight for you?"

A smile so bright it lit up the room spread across her face. "He did."

"How?"

"At prom. I had agreed to go with another boy. Someone my father approved of. Todd was there with a couple of his guy friends. He managed to get me alone and it was as if no time had passed. I loved him. He loved me."

"So you told your dad he couldn't boss you around?"

Grace laughed. "No, I did even better than that." Her eyes grew wet and she let out a sigh. "Todd proposed. He asked me to run away that night and marry him. At this point, we were both eighteen. Graduation was one week away, but we'd already completed all that was required of us."

"Grace! This is so romantic. You ran away with him?"

"Mm-hmm." Grace poured out seeds from the leaf packet onto her hand.

"What seeds are those?"

"Lettuce." Grace wiped her tears away. "Todd and I drove to Las Vegas and got married. When we came home a few days later, my dad was livid. He insisted we get the marriage annulled. I refused."

Grace again placed one seed in each of the little dirt cups as she spoke.

"My dad cut me off and threw me out of the house. He said he wasn't going to let that money-grubbing boy get his hands on any of his money."

"Oh no!"

"Todd didn't have any real skills. He couldn't get a job anywhere in town. My dad helped ensure that."

Lauren had been so worried about how controlling Nick was, but it didn't even compare to what her aunt had endured.

"Todd enlisted in the Army. He didn't ask me about it first. Just did it. I moved around with him from base to base, but I wasn't happy."

"Why didn't you go back home?"

Grace laughed. "I couldn't do that. That would

Chasing Her Trust

have been admitting my father was right. I would have never done that. No, I befriended the other Army wives and made the best of it. Todd was sent overseas for a tour. Then on our sixth wedding anniversary, there was a knock on my door."

"No."

Grace let the tears fall freely now.

"Todd died on the front line."

"Oh, Grace, I'm so sorry. Did you go home after that?"

She shook her head. "I called my mom and told her what happened. While she said she was sad about my circumstances, I couldn't come home. My father wouldn't budge in his decision."

"What did you do?"

Grace finished placing the seeds, then deposited the extras back in the packet.

"I said goodbye to all of the military wives, and I went out and made my own life."

"But you have a house in town. You have such nice things. How did...um..."

"You want to know where I got the money?" Grace grinned. "My father and I reconciled when he was on his deathbed. He finally admitted he'd been wrong, and he wrote me back into the will. After he passed, I was so bitter that I wouldn't touch his money or set foot in the house. It took years for me to come around."

"Grace, I'm sorry about William."

Grace reached for Lauren's hand. "Me too. This has been one shitty day."

Lauren stared at her aunt. She'd never heard her curse before.

"I need a drink." Grace turned to her. "Happy hour?"

At the mention of a drink, Lauren's stomach started doing flips. She watched Grace. No hint of sadness in her eyes.

Damn it, Nick. He was in her head and now she was suspecting the only family she had left.

"I'll have to pass on the drink. I just got released from the hospital."

Grace smacked her forehead. "Of course. How insensitive of me. I'm sorry. I'm afraid I'm not thinking straight today. You probably want to go to bed. Don't let me keep you up."

"Thank you." Lauren had taken a few steps when she remembered something Grace had said.

"Grace?"

"Yes?"

"Did you ever make the happy hour drinks for your husband?"

Grace stopped cleaning up the dirt and looked directly at Lauren. "No. He didn't drink." Then she smiled. "I'll see you in the morning. I'll cook up a big breakfast."

Breakfast. She felt uneasy about eating anything. But this was Grace. Could she really have tried to poison her?

    The will. Lauren needed to find that will. Then maybe she would have some answers.

Chapter Twenty-Six

The smell of bacon wafted into her room as she struggled to wake up. She checked her clock. It was almost lunchtime. Today would be her first day back at the diner since she got sick. Well, maybe sick or maybe poisoned. No one could tell her for sure.

Then Nick put just enough doubt in her mind about Grace that the smell of the food made her nauseated.

She threw on her robe and trudged downstairs.

"Good morning! Looks like you slept well."

Not at all. The argument she'd had with Nick had run through her head over and over. How had they gotten to that point?

"It was fine."

"I read through your discharge papers." Grace

Chasing Her Trust

scooped eggs and bacon onto a plate then set it down on the table. "It says you need to stay well-nourished and hydrated. Sit. Eat." She placed a fork and napkin next to the plate. "It also says to not overexert yourself, so you should stay home and rest today."

"Thank you. But as for the resting today, I'm due back at work."

Eyeing her plate of food, Lauren thought the odds the bacon would be poisoned were slim. She took a large bite of a strip. *Damn you, Nick!* Grace would never hurt her.

"No. Actually, you aren't," Grace said.

She swallowed the bacon. "What do you mean?"

Grace moved back to the stove and flipped what appeared to be a pancake.

"I called Logan this morning and explained you still needed rest. He understood and said someone would cover for you."

"Grace, no. The doctor said I would be fine to work today. You can't do that. I can't lose that job."

Grace turned and frowned. "I'm sorry, dear. I was looking out for you."

Of course she was. Grace had always been like another mother to her. And now they were all each other had. It was only natural that Grace might be a little overprotective.

"I know. Thank you for that. But I'll deal with Logan from now on, all right?"

Grace gave her shoulder a squeeze. "All right. Coffee? I made some."

Coffee made her think of Nick. Honestly, everything made her think of Nick. It hadn't even been twenty-four hours and she missed him.

"What's wrong?" Grace asked.

Lauren picked at the rest of the food on her plate, hoping Grace wouldn't notice she wasn't eating.

"I'm upset about Nick. I'm also upset about William. I had no idea he had health problems. It's all been a bit much. You know?"

Grace sat down and reached for Lauren's left hand. "I know. It has. A few months ago, I had a brother, a great sister-in-law, and a nephew. Now, here we are. We're all each other has left. I miss them terribly, but one thing I've learned in this life is that you can't wallow. You must move forward."

Lauren frowned at her food. She wasn't wallowing. She and Nick just broke up. She had the right to feel sad. And William had just passed. They couldn't simply forget him. Wait, why hadn't her aunt mentioned a service?

"Are you having a service for William?"

"A service?" Grace had jumped back up and was flipping more pancakes.

"A funeral?"

Grace stilled but didn't respond.

"Grace?"

Chasing Her Trust

Her aunt turned; a smile plastered on her face. "There will be a service in Portland next weekend. That's where his friends are. You're welcome to attend."

William's friends. She couldn't picture them. Her stepbrother wasn't exactly the warm and friendly type. But he was a CEO and must have had many business contacts. That would make the service more of a networking event than a grieving service. None of that appealed to her at all.

"Would you mind if I skipped it?"

"Not at all. I understand. You two weren't particularly close." Grace moved a few pancakes from the pan to a plate.

"Would you like a pancake?" her aunt asked without turning around.

"No, thank you."

"Oh, I almost forgot! Your birthday is soon! Your thirtieth, right?"

Lauren couldn't fight her smile. All the years she'd known this family, Michael and Grace had always remembered her birthday. They'd always sent her an expensive gift. She hadn't minded at all. She hadn't had much growing up, so she really appreciated it.

"Yes, it is. Thank you for remembering."

"We should do something special. I'll figure out something." Grace's smile fell when she looked at Lauren's plate.

"Lauren, you need to eat to regain your strength. At least finish your bacon, then you can go back upstairs and get some sleep."

"Thank you for making breakfast, but I'm afraid I can't eat any more." She stood and reached for her plate.

Grace's hand on her wrist stopped her. "Leave it. I'll take care of it. Go rest."

"Thank you." Lauren made her way upstairs and her mind wandered back to Nick. If she had to stay here resting all day, she was going to drive herself crazy.

When she reached the top of the stairs, her gaze went directly to William's room. The door was closed. Looking over her shoulder, she could hear her aunt cleaning the dishes. For some reason, she wanted to see inside William's room. She'd never been in there. On her way down the hall, her phone rang from her room. Abandoning her idea, she raced to answer it.

Disappointment filled her when she saw it wasn't Nick. It was her boss. "Hello?"

"Look, I know your aunt said you need your rest, but is there any way you can come in for even half your shift? I can't find anyone to cover."

Getting out of this house was exactly what she needed. "I'll be there. I'm sorry my aunt called you. I told her that wasn't appropriate."

Logan chuckled. "It was weird, but in this

town, if a Chanler asks you to do something, you pretty much do it."

"I'll be there in thirty minutes."

"Thank you! I really appreciate this."

★ ★ ★

Lauren managed to get out of the house without running into Grace. For that, she was grateful. She wasn't up for explaining herself. Not that she should have to. She was a grown woman who was capable of making her own decisions.

Several hours into her shift, she was ready for a nap. Now she felt guilty. Grace had been right. She wasn't strong enough to work yet.

"Lauren?"

The unfamiliar voice came from behind her. When she turned from the counter, her eyes met the very blue eyes of one of the best-looking men she'd ever seen. He didn't hold a candle to Nick, but men like this didn't just wander through Fisher Springs. And how the hell did he know her name?

"Yes?"

He held out his hand. "I'm Luke. I'm an old friend of Nick's."

She shook his hand. "I'm sorry, he didn't mention you."

Luke grinned. "I'm sure he didn't." Then he

became very serious. "Do you have a minute?"

Well, this was odd. Lauren surveyed the restaurant. There were only two customers and they'd already received their meals.

"I can spare a minute."

She walked over to an empty booth and sat down. Luke took a seat across from her.

"First, Nick doesn't know I'm here and if he did, he'd kill me."

"Then why are you here?" She leaned back and crossed her arms.

He grinned. "He did say you were a spitfire. He wasn't lying."

She arched a brow. "I said I'd give you a minute. You better get to the point."

If Nick sent this guy in to gain her sympathy, she wasn't going to make it easy.

"Nick's a wreck. He called me last night, drunk out of his mind. Nick doesn't get drunk. He was at some hole in the wall bar near me. Thankfully, he let me drive him back to my place."

Tears threatened, then she remembered what he'd said to her. "I'm happy he has a good friend, but him being upset won't undo what he said."

Luke grimaced. "He told me about the money comment. Yeah, I get why you're mad, but you have to understand, Nick's really defensive when it comes to money."

"You think?"

Chasing Her Trust

"I've known Nick a long time. Our families have known each other a long time. We both grew up with money and it really fucked with our heads, you know? We never knew whether someone wanted to be around us because they liked us or because they liked what we had access to. I knew Nick's ex. She was a few years ahead of me in high school, but everyone knew who she was. She was one of those rich, mean girl types."

Luke sighed and turned his gaze to the window. "She really screwed him over. He thought she loved him, but actually, she only wanted his name and his family money."

"Nick told me what happened."

Luke leaned forward. "All right, then you can understand. Nick gave up on relationships. Hell, he'd shut almost everyone out. But last night, he told me about you. I think he panicked. If for a moment, he thought you were choosing money or status over him, yeah, he'd probably overreact."

"He didn't overreact. He jumped to conclusions."

Luke laughed. "That sounds like Nick. He usually thinks he knows more than everyone else. He needs someone who can keep that big head of his deflated."

She didn't even try to suppress her grin as she thought about the day they met. He'd been so sure of himself that he thought she'd fall at his feet just because he smiled at her. God, she was mad at him. But now...now she really missed him.

"Nick's a teddy bear. He puts up a good front. Most people think he's this arrogant, cocky cop. And in some ways, he is. But those are his walls. And by the looks of how drunk he got last night; I'd say you got past those walls."

At last, the tears made their escape and cascaded down her cheeks.

Luke stood up. "It looks like he got past your walls too. Think about calling him back."

"I appreciate you coming here to talk to me, but I can't. I just got out of one messed up relationship. I can't go headfirst into another one."

Luke let out a sigh. "I understand. But I hope you change your mind."

As Luke exited the diner, Scott came in.

"Who was that?" Scott asked.

"None of your business. Are you here to eat or harass me?"

"I'm here to win you back. I heard you finally realized the detective wasn't for you."

How the hell could he know that?

As if he'd read her mind, he added, "Grace stopped by the police station and told the chief. Harvey was there and overheard them, and he told me. Is it true?"

Lauren grabbed a menu from the hostess station and pushed it at him. "Again, something else that's none of your business."

Scott grabbed her arm and tugged her closer to him. "Losing William made it clear to me that we don't have time to waste. Lauren, we were good together. Remember?" His other hand wrapped around her waist.

"Why do you want me back? The way you treated me; it isn't love. So why?"

He released her, grinding his teeth and staring at her.

"At first I did it because William paid me to do it."

That wasn't what she was expecting. "William? Why would he care?"

"Honestly, I have no idea. He said he wanted you out of the house."

She closed her eyes. William hated her so much that he couldn't stand being under the same roof as her?

"Why now? You said *at first*. William's gone."

"When I saw you with that detective, it drove me crazy. I'm sorry about the social media post, but I was so crazy jealous. Now I know I can't see myself with anyone but you."

Scott leaned in to kiss her. How could he think she'd kiss him back?

The bell above the door jingled and she jumped away. Sweet relief. Harmony had walked in.

"Thank goodness you're here, Harmony. I've

got to go," Lauren told her.

"Lauren, wait!" Scott called to her.

"Scott, just the man I want to see. We need to talk," said Harmony.

Lauren grinned as she made her way to the back. She knew Harmony was stalling him so she could run out.

"Sorry, Logan, I've got to go. I think I pushed too hard today."

"Leaving early again?" he asked.

"I'm not feeling well."

Logan laughed. "It's a good thing I really like you. Also, I saw Scott come in. I get it. Go. I'll go have a chat with him."

"Thank you."

She made it out to her car, and for the first time in hours, she checked her phone. There were over thirty missed text messages. Butterflies danced in her stomach as she hoped they were from Nick. No, she had to stop wishing to hear from Nick. Like she told Luke, she needed space.

The messages were from Grace. The first ten were in all caps.

YOU'RE SUPPOSED TO BE RESTING! NOT SNEAKING OUT!

YOU WENT TO WORK, DIDN'T YOU? I CALLED LOGAN AND CONFIRMED, SO DON'T LIE.

I CAN'T BELIEVE YOU AREN'T

FOLLOWING DOCTOR'S ORDERS. DO YOU WANT A RELAPSE?

How the hell could going to work cause a relapse of poisoning? Of course, the discharge papers that Grace had didn't mention that. Nick had kept that document, hoping to get the chief to take him more seriously in his pursuit of William.

Glancing down at the messages, she saw that her aunt had continued after a break, but she'd turned the caps lock off.

Let's have an early birthday celebration tonight. Just the two of us. I'm make something special.

I'm throwing you a party. It's all set. My church is letting us use their banquet room. I'm so excited!

Her church? She goes to church? How did Lauren not know this?

I'll send out invitations tomorrow, so everyone has a couple of weeks' notice. Can't wait!

The rest of the texts were about whether she liked chocolate or vanilla cake, red or white wine, and so on.

She leaned her head back and groaned. As much as she didn't want to deal with Grace and twenty questions right now, she understood. Grace was grieving. Losing William so soon after her own brother was a lot to take. She'd learned herself that grief can make you say and do strange things. She had to give her aunt some leeway and support. Maybe if she explained to Grace that she'd been right and

Chasing Her Trust

Lauren should have stayed home to rest, she could get a few hours alone in her room before dinner.

Chapter Twenty-Seven

Nick pushed the door to the police station open. It had been nearly three weeks since he'd driven Lauren home. No texts. No calls. Not even an accidental sighting. He'd checked in with Harmony, who said Lauren was doing fine.

A few days after William died, Nick had received a call from the Portland officer. He'd unofficially gone into William's condo after his death as a favor to Nick. Turns out, William had an entire room dedicated to plants. He'd never thought William to be a green thumb, but at least it alleviated his fears that someone was still after Lauren.

After news of William's death got out, some men came to town asking around. Good old Zach got one of them drunk and found out William owed six figures in debts to the wrong men. Once they discovered William was dead, they left.

As Nick sat at the station on another slow day, his mind kept drifting to Lauren as it always did. After Luke fessed up that he went to see her, Nick held out an ounce of hope. That was until Luke told him what she said. She didn't want him.

Could he really move on? It had been weeks and he couldn't stop thinking about her and trying to figure out what he could do to make this right.

Last week, before he'd heard from the Portland officer, he snuck back into the mansion when he was sure Grace and Lauren were gone. Part of him hoped he would run into Lauren. That he could apologize, and they could pick up where they left off.

But she wasn't there. Fortunately, however, the new urn was up on the mantle next to the others. He grabbed a sample of William's ashes and got out of there. After that, he drove by Grace's house but didn't seen any evidence of a garden. And the greenhouse on the property was empty. He realized then that maybe William had died of a heart attack. Yet the thought didn't make him feel any better. No, only getting those ashes checked would.

While he knew what he discovered wouldn't be admissible in court, he had to find out if Lauren was truly in danger.

"Hey, Nick. How are you feeling?" Harvey was leaning back in his chair, boots up on his desk, wearing a shit-eating grin.

Harvey didn't smile at him. Something was up.

"Feeling fine." He tried to make his way to his desk, but Harvey was fast and was already standing in his path.

"I'm sorry you and Lauren didn't work out, but you know it's for the best, right? She's Scott's girl."

"Why the hell are you bringing this up now?"

"Because it looks like Lauren went back to Scott. Figured someone should tell you before you run into them."

Nick took a deep breath. Harvey was trying to bait him. He knew Lauren wouldn't do that.

"I doubt she'd give him the time of day." Nick finally pushed past him and made his way to his chair.

"Oh yeah? Then explain this." Harvey held up his phone. It was open to a photo of Scott and Lauren. His arms were around her, and they were standing in a restaurant that was decked out with holiday decor and he could see the Christmas tree in the background. It was recent.

"Ms. Finkle says she took that three weeks ago but didn't have the heart to tell you. Good thing I do."

Three weeks ago. She wouldn't go back to him, would she?

Nick fell into his chair and avoided eye contact with Harvey. He couldn't let that prick see that he'd gotten to him.

"Lauren's free to do what she wants. You get any calls today?"

"Nope." Harvey answered and made his way over to his desk, where he began playing games on his phone.

Damn it, Lauren. Why would you go back to him?

His cell phone rang. He silenced it, then walked to the door. "Hey, I'm going to get some air. I'll be right back."

Harvey chuckled. "Yeah, take all the time you need. I understand."

Asshole. But at least it bought him time to return this call.

"Johnson, thank you for doing this. It's good to know I can still count on the county lab when I need it."

"You owe me for this one, by the way. My boss doesn't appreciate me calling in favors."

"Yeah, but there's a woman who could be in danger. I had to know."

"I just emailed you the lab results. The test came back negative. But they only tested for a handful of toxins."

"You mean they can't test for plants?"

"No, not from ashes. Did you get a chance to see if anyone has a greenhouse or is growing oleander? This sounds like that old case we worked on."

It was exactly like that case.

"It turns out, William had a green thumb. I only have photos and I can't tell if any of his plants are oleander. Do you mind taking a look?"

"Sure, send them over. But my money's not on William."

Nick frowned. "Why not?"

"After talking to you, I did a little background check on Grace. Did you know she was once married?"

"No, but I don't really know her."

"Well, she was. And her husband died of a heart attack."

"How did you get to those kinds of records?"

"Google."

"Really?"

"Yeah. Maybe I should have been the detective," Johnson laughed.

"Ha ha. Well, no wonder Grace quickly dealt with William's body. Probably too much of a reminder."

"Or she was hiding evidence."

"You think she poisoned her husband?" Nick turned around and stared into the windows of the police station. Harvey was still sitting at his desk playing video games on his phone. He would love to throw Harvey into the county sheriff's office. He wouldn't get away with any of his shit.

"Grace's husband died when he was twenty-five. I spoke with his family and they all said his death had come as a shock. He'd been healthy and never got sick. Then, out of the blue, he had a heart attack."

"It happens."

"His brother said the family never felt like they got to say goodbye. Apparently, Grace had the body cremated less than twenty-four hours after he died."

That uneasy feeling returned.

"That's a strong coincidence."

Please don't let it be Grace. Lauren needs her.

"It is. So I dug some more. I'll email everything I have, and you can see if you reach the same conclusion."

"Thanks."

"Oh, one more thing. The results on the whiskey test came back."

"Yeah?"

"It's just whiskey."

★ ★ ★

"Detective, are you serious right now?"

Judge Milton glared at Nick as he stood before him holding the warrant he needed him to sign.

"I'm very serious."

"I know you're new here, so maybe you don't understand, but I can't have you go tearing up that poor woman's house. She's grieving for God's sake! I don't know what kind of evidence you think you have on her, but she is a beloved member of this community. And two days before Christmas, no less?"

"Your Honor—"

"Your Honor, we need that warrant." The chief burst into the courtroom and marched up to the judge. "I'm fully aware of what Detective Moore is requesting, and he has the full support of the police department."

Thank you, Chief. Nick had texted the chief explaining all that he found, but he wasn't sure if he would support him. Dunin hadn't been into the office for them to discuss it in person.

"Damn it, Dunin. Are you sure?"

"Sadly, I am. I received a copy of her husband's death certificate. He died of a heart attack en route to a Seattle hospital. Apparently, Grace told everyone he died in the line of duty."

"Well, she elaborated, probably for sympathy. I don't see how that's enough."

"The man was twenty-five. Also, as Nick probably already shared with you, Mr. Chanler and Ms. Harrow also died of heart attacks."

"Chief, they were on vacation in another country."

"Yes, but Grace had flown to the same country the day before they died. She left the next morning."

The judge leaned back. "She flew in, then flew

out hours later?"

"Yes."

Nick stepped up. "That's four heart attacks, plus Ms. Chanler raced both William and her husband's bodies through to cremation before any tests could be run. That's enough for probable cause for the warrant."

The judge ran his hands over his face. "Damn it. I'll sign the warrant. But if you don't find anything, you will leave that woman alone. Understood?"

"Yes, Your Honor," the chief said.

The moment the warrant was in Nick's hands, he raced out of the courtroom. The chief was right behind him.

"I'm calling Harvey in on this too." The chief pulled out his phone and told Harvey to meet them at Grace's house.

There were no cars in the driveway when they arrived. Nick was the first one to the door, so he pounded on it.

Harvey pulled up and joined them on the porch. After no one answered, the chief unlocked the door.

Nick arched a brow.

"Grace gave me a key a few years ago. I've never used it."

"Why did she give you a key?"

"After my wife died, she started flirting with me. She's a nice woman, but I wasn't ready. Anyway, let's go."

The home was a one-story that sprawled across a property with beautiful landscaping. After circling the house and not finding a single plant, the chief shrugged. "I guess we were wrong."

Nick's gut said they were missing something. "We weren't wrong. We have to look harder."

They tried every door, but none led to a basement.

Harvey began pulling at the carpet.

"What the hell are you doing, Harvey?" the chief asked.

"Looking for an opening."

Harvey walked the perimeter, pulling on the carpet.

"He's right. If she does have something to hide, she's going to conceal it."

Nick went back to the hallway, where the bedrooms were located. The chief and Harvey followed.

"I was once inside this house where a bookcase much like the one here" — he gestured at the wooden bookcase they were standing beside — "was actually a door into another room."

With that, Nick pushed on it and it moved back on the right. He then continued pushing on the right side, and it swung open to expose a small, brightly lit room. Under the lights were a variety of plants.

Nick pulled up a photo of the suspected plant on his phone and walked slowly past each one.

A moment later, Harvey was by his side. "What are we looking for?"

"Oleander. It looks like this." Nick held up a photo he'd gotten off the internet.

They all searched.

"Damn it," the chief said, and Nick and Harvey turned toward him. "Here it is."

They walked over to the chief, who pointed to the back row. There were at least ten oleander plants.

The chief turned to Nick. "All right. Here are your plants. Now how will you prove she did this? You told me yourself the lab can't test someone's ashes for this toxin."

"Lauren. I'm positive she poisoned Lauren. We can get her tested."

"She was sick weeks ago. I doubt it's still in her system," The chief said.

Fuck. He was right. "What other choice do we have than to ask her to get tested?" Nick asked.

The chief's hands went to his hips. "We don't. You can ask her, but don't tip off Grace."

Ask Lauren? He hadn't spoken to her in weeks and now he was going to ask her to voluntarily get tested because he thought her aunt tried to kill her. Yeah, that would go over well.

Chapter Twenty-Eight

"Yes, Walter. Thank you for letting me know."

Grace was on the phone when Lauren got home from work. She'd been imagining soaking in a tub of Epsom salts to sooth her sore feet. She'd figured it would get busy this time of year, but she'd never imagined it would be this busy. Only two days until Christmas, and then, hopefully, everything would calm down.

Two days. That meant one day until her birthday. From what she'd heard at the diner, Grace was moving full steam ahead with the party plans. People she'd never met were coming. It sounded more like a holiday party than a birthday party. Someone said even Santa Claus would be there. It didn't matter, she knew one person that wouldn't be there — Nick.

She'd told herself to give it time, things would get easier. She'd gone back and forth about whether she'd overreacted or not. Harmony had been her sounding board and was firmly on Team Nick. She was convinced Lauren was too scared to pursue something real. The more time that passed, the more she wondered if her friend was right. She couldn't stop thinking about him.

Grace turned to see Lauren as she slammed the phone down, her eyes wide and her skin pale.

"Walter? Is that a boyfriend?"

"Boyfriend? No, Walter Milton is an old friend. He had some disturbing news."

"What's wrong?" Lauren took Grace's hand, but Grace immediately withdrew it.

"This was supposed to be easy," Grace said. "Why did you have to make it so hard?"

Her aunt's expression was vacant as she stared past Lauren.

"Make what hard?"

Grace shook her head. "I need your help with something."

Her aunt raced to a drawer in the kitchen and pulled out a box of matches. Then she grabbed a stack of papers from the counter and held the items out to Lauren.

"I need you to go start a fire in the fire pit right now. Okay?"

She took everything from her aunt, confused.

"We have a fire pit?"

"Yes, you can see it from the back porch. Please hurry."

Lauren glanced out the window. "But it's dark outside. Can't this wait until morning?"

"No, we must do it now. Hurry!" Grace ran up the stairs. She'd never seen Grace run, but everything about her demeanor told Lauren she needed to get the fire going fast.

She flipped the light switch that illuminated the entire back porch. Once outside, she found the fire pit and some wood in a shed nearby. She stacked a few logs and lit some of the crumpled paper and the fire took off. She reached for more paper from the pile, and that's when she saw it. "The Last Will and Testament of Michael Chanler."

When she looked behind her at the house, there was no sign of Grace. She opened the document and quickly scanned through it. This was the first time she'd seen it. She must have left her copy at the apartment with Scott.

On the next to last page, it referenced a trust. She dug into the pile and there was another document titled "Trust."

She scanned the documents until she saw her name. She'd never taken the time to read any of this. Her mother had signed a prenup, so Lauren had been certain there was nothing for her anyway. But there it was. Michael had left the house to her as long as she was living there on her thirtieth birthday. If she chose not to live there, the house would go to his son, William.

Why would he leave the house to me and why on my thirtieth birthday?

Michael had been older than her mom and it was known that he had heart problems. But still, the short timeline struck her as odd.

The back door opened, and Lauren turned to face the fire. She shoved the papers half down her pants and then pulled her sweater over the rest. She needed to get alone to read this.

"Thank you so much. That fire is great."

"My mom and I went camping a lot when I was younger. She taught me."

Grace stepped up beside her holding a banker's box.

"Your mother was a great woman. I'm sorry about what happened to them."

Tears welled in Lauren's eyes. She needed to change the subject.

"Why the urgency with the fire?"

Grace removed the lid to the box. It was full of paper.

"I've been meaning to shred these documents for a long time. I figured a fire would be better. I love bonfires. Don't you?"

Grace had a smile plastered on her face. She set the entire box into the fire pit.

"It might burn better if you throw the papers in separately," Lauren suggested.

"No time."

"No time? Is someone coming?" Lauren looked back to the house.

Grace laughed nervously. "No, I just meant we were losing daylight."

Living in the Pacific Northwest in December meant they'd lost daylight nearly an hour ago.

"Are you feeling all right?"

Grace turned to Lauren. "Never better. You ready for dinner? I made stew."

The papers cut into her stomach, reminding her she needed to be alone.

"Sure. I'm going to go clean up first. Since I just got home from work, I feel greasy. You know, working in a diner."

"Okay, but don't take too long. The food's getting cold."

"All right."

Lauren walked as fast as she could to the house. On the way through the kitchen, she saw the crockpot on the counter. It was turned on high. High. How could dinner be getting cold?

She ran up the stairs and locked her door.

Before she could read the papers, her phone rang. Nick. The sight of his name made her tingle with happiness. God, what a mess she'd made of everything with him. But she needed him now.

"Nick—"

"Lauren, can you come to the station? We'd like you to consent to a blood test. We have reason to believe Grace poisoned William."

She sank down on the bed, and the pit in her stomach grew. "Something's going on here. I'm not sure I can leave."

"Is Grace there?"

"Yes, and she's acting strange. She's burning documents in the back yard."

"I need you to get out of there. Now. Make up any excuse."

"Why?"

"I believe you're in danger."

The pit in her stomach doubled in size at his words. "Where are you?"

"On my way. I'll be there soon."

"Lauren?" Grace called from downstairs.

Lauren unlocked and opened her door. "I'm upstairs. Still cleaning up."

"Can you help me really quick? I burned myself in the fire."

Lauren frowned. If Grace was actually hurt, she needed to help her. When she made her way downstairs, she discovered the front door was open and the kitchen light was off.

What the hell?

"Grace?"

"Why couldn't you have had the stew that

Chasing Her Trust

night? Then I wouldn't' be forced to do this!"

Grace came out of the kitchen, and a gleam of light caught Lauren's eye just before Grace raised her arm and lunged at her with a butcher knife. Lauren dodged it, but it caught on her sweater and ripped it before she hurried out the front door.

Once outside in the darkness, she wasn't sure where to go, so she ran up the driveway.

She'd made it about two hundred feet when headlights came on behind her and the sound of a car accelerating caused her to jump behind a line of trees.

"Why do you keep making this so hard?" Grace screamed from the driver's window, and as Lauren tried to circle behind the car and run toward the house, the reverse lights came on and it barreled toward her.

Before Lauren could figure out where to go next, flashing lights and sirens were speeding down the driveway. She circled back to the tree line and as she raced toward the police car, it stopped, and Nick got out of the passenger side.

"Grace is trying to kill me! She tried to run me down."

When she turned around, Grace's car door was open, and she'd made it halfway across the field.

"Wait here," Nick said and took off in pursuit, then the chief stepped out of the driver's side of the police car.

"What's going on?" Lauren asked.

"We finally got a copy of the will and trust of Michael Chanler about twenty minutes ago. It looks like you were meant to be the heir to all of this as long as you're living here on your thirtieth birthday."

"What if I wasn't living here? Then who would get it?"

"I'll let Nick fill you in on all of that. It gets complicated."

"Chief, are you there?" someone called out through his walkie-talkie.

The chief pulled it off his belt. "Go ahead, Harvey."

"I got waylaid by a cow in the road. I'll be there in a few minutes."

The chief went back to his car. "Okay. Get here as soon as you can."

At that moment, Lauren heard footsteps coming up behind her and she spun around.

"This is my house, bitch!" Grace screamed. "You can't come waltzing in and take what has been part of my family for generations!" Then she raised her hand, which still held the butcher knife, and the realization that her aunt, the woman who'd been like a mother to her, wanted to kill her crushed Lauren. But why? Grace had her own money. It didn't make any sense.

"Grace"—the chief was by Lauren's side, his gun aimed at Grace—"I don't know what's going on, but you need to put that knife down."

Grace shook her head and wiped her eyes with her free hand. "No, don't you see? Now she's going to get it all. All of it, Ross. It was supposed to be mine. Daddy said he'd change his will back. But then he left it all to Michael. Michael didn't deserve all of this."

Grace fell to her knees. "I deserved all of this. Ross, you know me. You know I deserved all of this."

Grace raised the knife and pointed it toward herself.

"No!" The chief lunged just as the knife was about to enter her stomach and when he knocked it away, Grace fell on her side. The chief then rolled her onto her stomach and pulled her arms behind her back.

"Grace Chanler, you are under arrest for the attempted murder of Lauren Harrow...."

Chapter Twenty-Nine

Nick ran out from the trees where he'd gone to chase Grace. His eyes were on Lauren as he scanned her body. "Are you all right?"

She nodded.

A second police car pulled up and Harvey got out.

"Just a second," Nick went to Harvey and said something. Harvey nodded, then Nick came back. "Harvey agreed to wait for the sheriff's deputies to arrive to help them with the investigation. I need to get you out of here to get your statement. Can we drive your car?"

That's when Lauren noticed the chief had taken Grace away. The reality of what had happened started to sink in.

"Yes. My keys are inside the house."

Chasing Her Trust

"I'll get them."

Nick returned and opened the passenger door for her. "I'll drive, okay?"

She nodded. She was in no state to even try. Her mind was going a million miles a second.

Once Nick was in the car, he turned to her. "I never asked, but I always wanted to know something."

Her heart rate kicked up a few notches.

"Why do you have a stuffed llama in your car?"

That was not what she was expecting. Unable to stop herself, she barked out a laugh. And he must have at least seen the humor, because he grinned.

"It was the last thing my mom bought me before she passed away. She said she got it on some vacation they went on. Now I have it with me wherever I go."

"That's very sweet."

Lauren nodded. "I always wanted a pet llama growing up. My mom saw it and remembered."

As they drove in silence, her mind jumped from her mom to Grace. Had Grace shown any signs that she wanted Lauren gone?

"Have you had a chance to read the will yet?" Nick asked, pulling her from her thoughts.

She reached into her pants and pulled out the crumpled papers. "Grace was trying to burn this. I was only able to scan it. I saw my name in the trust, but I didn't fully understand."

"The chief got a copy, and according to Mr. Chanler's attorney, he was concerned for your well-being. There was a note in the file from Michael to you. The attorney thought he'd sent it with your copy, but it was somehow overlooked."

Nick handed her the letter. "You can read it later if you'd like privacy."

"Thank you. Maybe it will explain why me. My mom signed a prenup. He barely knew me."

"According to his attorney, he really loved your mom and you as well. He wanted to make sure you were cared for."

"But what about William? He's the logical heir."

"William was wealthy on his own, or so everyone thought."

Michael really loved her mom. She'd wondered if he had, because he never showed much emotion when she was around. The fact that her mom had finally found love made her smile.

"The trust was set up so that you'd have the right to this house, but only after you turned thirty. There were some other stipulations."

"I'll be thirty tomorrow."

"Yes, and that's likely why Grace became so frantic. If you hadn't been living here, then the house would've reverted to William."

"But William died. Wait, what would've

happened to the house if William hadn't been able to take it?"

"The trust didn't list anyone else. It would've then gone into probate and under state laws, it would've gone to the next of kin. But Mr. Chanler had no other children and no living parents."

"So Grace would've gotten it."

During those few summer visits, Lauren couldn't recall Grace ever being at this house. Now that she considered it, she and her mom always met Grace at whatever place they were all going to. How had she not remembered that? Although why would she have thought anything of it? Michael was often busy at work and she simply thought shopping was Grace's way of having fun.

"I don't recall Grace ever being in this house before her brother passed. Why did she want it so badly?"

"I don't know. Maybe she thought she'd get the money too. Hopefully, the chief can get those answers. You'll need to give a statement, but we don't have to go to the station. Grace will be there."

"What money?"

Nick grinned. "Well Ms. Harrow, it turns out, you are a very rich woman. You just didn't know it."

Nick reiterated what the attorney had told him about the money as they drove to an apartment building on the other side of town.

"Where are we?" she asked.

"My apartment," Nick said. "Once word got out we split, an apartment opened up."

Her stomach clenched. Where Nick lived. He had a whole life she knew nothing about now. God, she missed him. She wanted his arms around her, comforting her.

"Is this all right?" he asked.

She nodded.

He shut off the engine, but neither of them moved.

"Grace mentioned her dad cut her out of his will. She told me she'd run off with a guy he didn't approve of." She shivered.

Snow had started to fall. Tomorrow was her birthday. Then Christmas. And she'd never felt more alone in this world. Tears fell from the corners of her eyes.

Then Nick's hand was on her arm. It brought back all the feelings she missed.

"Let's go inside," he said.

They walked through the parking lot in silence. He opened the door and she went in. She wasn't sure what she was expecting, but this wasn't it. The apartment almost looked vacant.

"Do you have furniture?"

He smiled. "I have a bed and dresser. That's all I need right now."

The lack of furniture was another reminder of how he thought of this as a temporary assignment.

"Do you still plan to leave in a few months?" She stepped further in. There wasn't even a hand towel in the kitchen.

"Depends."

She turned to ask him more, but when his gaze met hers, she couldn't breathe. The longing in his eyes matched what she felt. He swallowed then broke their spell by looking away.

"There are a couple of barstools." He sat on one and pulled out his phone. "Do you mind if I record this statement?"

She shook her head as she sat on the other stool.

He placed his phone between them and turned on a recording app.

"Let's start from this morning. Were you home?"

She shook her head.

"Please answer yes or no." He pointed to the phone.

She recounted her day, including Grace's strange behavior. When she finished, he turned off the recorder but didn't move.

"I'm sorry," Nick said as he stared at the counter. "What I said in the car was wrong. It was hurtful. I got scared and defensive."

She could barely breathe. She didn't move, hoping he would say more.

He reached for her hand and she didn't pull it

back. "When you insisted on staying in that house, it triggered something."

His fingers caressed hers. "My ex cared more about money and status than anything else. When you picked the house over what I thought was your safety, for a moment, I thought maybe you were like her in that way."

"Nick, in that moment, I didn't think I was in danger in that house with Grace. She was the closest thing I had to a mom at that point and I wanted to be with her."

He nodded. "I see that now. I misjudged you and I'm so sorry."

He lifted his gaze and their eyes met. "I've missed you so much. I wanted to talk to you many times, but I was tied up in this case and I had no idea what to say. I hoped you'd come back to me. But now I realize I need to fight for you, for us."

Hope bloomed inside her chest. Maybe there was hope this could be saved. She placed her other hand on his and squeezed. "I've missed you too."

* * *

"Wait just a second." Nick jumped up and went to his bedroom.

He'd been debating whether this was a good idea for the last week, but he had to let Lauren know he truly had been thinking about her.

He reached into his closet and pulled out the box. When he walked back toward the kitchen, he stopped. Lauren was leaning forward on the counter, deep in thought. Despite all she went through tonight, she was so beautiful, it took his breath away.

As he approached, she turned those amber eyes to him.

"I got you something. For your birthday. I saw it and thought of you." He placed it in front of her.

She undid the ribbon and slowly opened the box. Her jaw dropped as she took in the pen and letter opener set.

"It's not the most romantic, but I remember you said you wanted to get back to accounting and I—"

"I love it." Her eyes welled with tears. "And it's engraved."

He'd had her name and "Best accountant ever" engraved on both items.

"Thank you."

She jumped into his arms and he held her tight. How the hell did he ever think she was materialistic? He'd given her a small gift and she was happy.

He leaned his forehead against hers.

"Happy birthday, Lauren. In a few short hours, you'll be the new owner of the Chanler mansion."

Chasing Her Trust

"I can't believe it."

"I know it's been a crazy day, and if you don't want to talk about this tonight, I'll understand, but I'd really like to take you out for dinner. Like a date."

"I'd like that." She smiled up at him, and seeing her smile again brought back all his want and need for his woman.

He leaned down and softly kissed her.

"Detective, I hope you missed me more than that."

Her hand was on his chest. She gripped his shirt and pulled him into a deeper kiss. All their feelings seemed to explode at once.

Their hands were everywhere, pulling at each other's clothing in a frenzy. He backed them into his bedroom, leaving behind a mess of clothes thrown all over his floor. When the back of his knees hit his bed, she pushed him down.

He propped himself up on his elbows and watched as she climbed on and straddled him, wearing only her bra and panties. As her lips nipped at his jaw, he got a firm grasp on her hips and guided her to grind against him.

"Oh fuck, that feels so good. I've missed how good you feel," he breathed out as she bumped and gyrated.

"I know something that might feel better." She scooted off him before he could ask, taking his boxer briefs with her as she went. Then her hand clasped around his length and she began to stroke him.

Lying back, he tried his hardest not to come after two pumps. But then he felt her hot, wet tongue on his tip. When he lifted his head to watch, she took him into her mouth and practically swallowed his entire length.

"You have to stop or I'm going to come."

She released him from her mouth with and audible pop. "I'd like that."

"No, I need to be inside you tonight." He tugged on her arm and she crawled up his body.

"Have you been with anyone since me?" he asked.

"No."

"Neither have I. Any chance you're on the pill?"

She nodded and understood what he was asking. "I want to feel all of you, with nothing between us," she said.

Standing up, she slowly peeled off her panties, then climbed back on top of him. His hands went to her back and unclasped her bra. The moment her breasts were free, his mouth was on them, licking and sucking.

While he was busy with her breasts, she lined him up and in one move she had him fully seated inside her. They both groaned. He'd never felt anything this good.

When she swiveled her hips, he knew he

wouldn't last long.

Reaching his arms around her, he lifted her and flipped them both then laid her on her back. He entered her slowly. Never breaking eye contract, he drove into her over and over. He wanted her to see him loving her. With their gazes locked, the energy shifted. He wanted her to know how he felt about her.

He moved his hand between them, pinching her clit, and she gasped. "Oh God, Nick, that feels incredible." Continuing to rub it in a circular motion, he worked her until her body tensed, and he knew she was close. His lips crashed down on hers and as he claimed her mouth, he applied more pressure with his fingers.

The moment her orgasm hit, she gripped his shoulders hard, fingernails digging deep. As her pussy clamped down on his cock, he couldn't hold back any longer and went over the edge with her.

Once they'd both caught their breath, he kissed her gently.

"I'll be right back."

He went to the bathroom and returned with a warm washcloth. After gently cleaning her up, he pulled her to him. He couldn't stop kissing her. He'd missed this woman more than he ever thought possible.

"Ready for that date?" he asked.

She smiled. "Why don't we order something in?"

"Pizza all right?"
"Perfect."

Chapter Thirty

Two weeks later.

Lauren would never get sick of the sight of Nick walking into the diner, smiling at her as if she was everything.

"I'm happy everyone backed off about Scott," Harmony said as she stood next to Lauren.

"I bet not happier than me."

She was more concerned with whether Grace would go to prison. Over the past two weeks, Grace had told lie after lie to the police. At first, she'd tried to lead everyone to believe William had been behind making Lauren sick. She gave a statement that implicated Scott, saying Scott believed that if he couldn't have Lauren, no one should. This caused Scott to come forward and say it was all a lie. And he ended up admitting to having a deal with William to lure Lauren away from the house for money.

Once everyone learned Scott hadn't loved her and only wanted money, they finally stopped pushing them together. She never thought it was possible Scott wouldn't be viewed as perfect.

Nick continued to have some trouble fitting in. Many in the town still believed Joey should be the detective. It amazed her that for a small town, how few knew the truth about him.

"Hey, babe." Nick gave her a toe-curling kiss.

One customer in the back let out a wolf whistle.

"I missed you," she said when she pulled away. She almost felt silly since they'd just seen each other that morning, but, damn it, she did miss him.

"I missed you too. Are you almost ready?" He leaned down and kissed her again.

"Five minutes."

He nodded. "I'll wait at the counter."

Lauren got the check ready for her last customer and then went to the back to grab her purse. Harmony was sitting in a chair near the lockers and staring into space while clutching her phone.

"Harmony, are you all right?"

Her friend turned to her, a smile on her face. "I'm good."

"Uh oh." Lauren knew that look.

"What?"

"What's his name?"

Harmony snapped out of her daydream. "What? No, there's no guy. I'm just tired."

Lauren narrowed her eyes. "You forget how well I know you."

"Don't you have your own guy to think about? Don't worry about me. We'll talk later." Harmony gave her a hug and then went out to the front.

Lauren was so appreciative of her friendship with Harmony. She'd lucked out when she moved to Fisher Springs and met Harmony that first day.

Once she and Nick were outside, he announced, "I have news."

"Sounds ominous."

He nodded. "Grace gave a full confession in exchange for a plea deal."

A pit formed in her stomach. "What kind of deal?"

"The offer was for twenty years in exchange for a full confession."

"Twenty years? That's longer than I expected. And how do they know her confession was real this time?"

The chief walked up. "Good afternoon, Lauren. Nick."

"Chief," Nick said.

"Chief, how do you know Grace's latest confession is the truth? Why do you believe her this time?" Lauren asked.

The chief glanced at Nick. "You should tell her."

"What's going on?" Lauren eyed them both.

Nick's arm wrapped around her shoulder. "Well, it turns out, Grace is guilty of more than just trying to kill you. While we suspected this all along, we had no proof. Until now."

"What else did she do?"

Nick rocked back on his heels.

"Once Grace started talking, she wouldn't stop. Not only did she confess to trying to poison you, but when the officer asked her why she thought the poison would work, she said because she'd done it several times before."

Lauren's stomach dropped. She'd been living with a murderer and never suspected a thing. She hadn't really known Grace at all. "Several times?"

Nick pulled her closer to him. "She said she'd poisoned William, Michael, and your mother."

Her knees gave out, and Nick caught her as she went down.

"No, they died on vacation. I was told in a car accident."

"Who told you?" the chief asked.

"I need to sit down."

Nick helped her to the bench outside the diner.

Chief Dunin cleared his throat, then spoke. "After Grace confessed, I looked into how your mom and Michael died. They were at a resort in the

Caribbean and the official cause of death was heart attack. But for some reason no one down there found it odd that two people would die of a heart attack at the same time."

She shook her head. "No. There's no way."

Nick squeezed her hand. "I called in a favor from a buddy I went to boot camp with. Long story short, Grace flew into that country the day before they died," Nick said.

"When did she leave?" she asked.

"The next morning. Your mom and Michael weren't discovered until that afternoon when housekeeping entered the room," Nick explained.

Tears streamed down her face. The woman who was like a mother to her had killed her real mother. But why? "Why would Grace do that?"

"Grace was broke. Michael was paying her a monthly allowance to keep her in her home, but she wanted more," the chief said.

Lauren shook her head. "But she told me she reconciled with her dad before he died, and he put her back in the will. She should have had money."

The chief continued to explain. "No, she didn't. Everything—the house, the business, the money—all went to Michael. Grace was completely cut out."

"What about her mom?"

Dunin shook his head. "Grace's mom died when Grace was in her twenties. She didn't take it well. Never recovered, actually." He scratched his beard. "Then after their father died, Michael and Grace didn't speak for years. But according to Michael's longtime friend, they reconciled, and Michael agreed to make Grace his sole heir."

"He cut his son out?"

"William had made millions in his own right. His father felt he was fine on his own. Apparently, before William got caught up in gambling, he was doing quite well," the chief told her.

"Gambling?"

"Evidently, he'd had a problem for years."

This didn't make sense. "Michael must have changed his will then."

"Yes, after he married your mother. It appears he never told Grace. But as you know, she got a copy of his will after he died. That must have been when her second plan came into play," the chief said.

Lauren leaned against the brick wall. "But why didn't she kill me? She killed William and I lived with her for weeks and I'm still here."

The chief swallowed. "I asked her that. She explained she had to wait so it didn't seem suspicious. Her plan was to make it look like you were in a car accident on your birthday."

Lauren shook her head. "How the hell would that have worked?"

"It wouldn't have. You saw her that night. She was spiraling out of control."

Lauren turned to Nick. "But you knew she was

Chasing Her Trust

guilty. You saved me."

Nick took her hands. "We all did. Harvey and the chief were there too."

"I still can't believe this. Grace was like a mother to me. She was kind and looked after me these last few weeks. Was her house not enough for her?"

The chief shook his head. "Actually, the house wasn't hers. That house she claimed was hers was a rental and Michael had been paying the rent a couple of months in advance. Grace failed to keep up and the owner started the eviction process. She always saw the mansion as hers. I never realized how far she'd go to take ownership of it. I'm sorry you had to go through this Lauren," the chief said.

"Chief, you there?"

Dunin grabbed his walkie-talkie from his belt. "Go ahead, Harvey."

"We have a situation. Looks like the Mertz goats escaped again. They're running down Slater Road."

The chief sighed. "Be right there."

Nick smiled. "I'm happy to see I'm not the only one getting those types of calls."

Dunin laughed. "Welcome to a small town. I better get going."

"Need any help?" Nick asked.

"No. I'm known as the goat whisperer around here. I'll get them rounded up. Enjoy your day."

Once the chief had left, Nick took her hand.

"Did you ever read that letter from Michael?"

"I did."

"Did it provide you with any answers?"

She smiled, remembering the sweet words Michael had written explaining why he'd left her the house and why she had to be living there on her thirtieth birthday.

"It did. It turns out, Michael had cancer and didn't have long to live. His plan was to give me the house outright, but my mom had requested he put in the clause that I had to live in the house with no houseguests. He explained she didn't like Scott and she'd hoped that time away from him would be a wake-up call for me."

"Is that so? Your mom was a smart woman."

"You would have liked her."

"If she was anything like you, then I'm sure I would have." He leaned down and kissed her.

"I have news." Lauren jumped up, excited to tell him. "*Somehow*, Zach Brannigan found out I was an accountant."

"That's interesting," Nick grinned.

"And it happens, his accountant is moving away at the end of this month. He asked me if I would take over."

"That's great!"

"It would only be a part-time gig, but if I do a good job and he tells others, I might be able to have my own accounting business."

"That's wonderful. You better get business cards made up so Zach can hand them out."

"Great idea."

"Do you have a name for your business yet?"

A smile stretched across her face. "Harrow Accounting."

Epilogue

Eleven months later.

Nick grabbed his jacket from the back of his chair.

"You really gonna do this, Moore?"

Nick spun around to see Harvey smiling at him. "Yes. And then I hope I don't get called out tonight."

"Life in a small town. You're always on duty. You miss the big city?"

Nick chuckled. "I thought I would, but no, I don't. How about you? You want to leave this place?"

Harvey laughed. "Sorry to break it to you, Moore, but you're going to have to compete with me for chief of this town."

Harvey held up his fist and Nick shook his head and bumped it. They'd come so far from that first meeting.

"What are your plans later tonight?"

Harvey's cheeks flushed. *Interesting.* Both he and Lauren had suspected he was seeing someone but keeping it a secret.

"Oh, you know, I'll just relax at home. It's a holiday weekend, so most people are with family."

Nick leaned in closer. "You ready to reveal who she is yet?"

"What?" Harvey took a step back. "Who *who* is?"

Nick couldn't hide the grin on his face. He already had a pretty good idea, but he wasn't going to share it with Lauren. That wasn't for him to tell.

Harvey shook his head. "That obvious, huh?"

"Yep."

"She's someone special, but I haven't told her how I feel."

"Why not?"

Harvey grinned. "She's a friend and I'm not sure she wants to cross that line, you know?"

"Well, you'll never know if you don't ask."

"Yeah, I did kiss her once."

"Oh yeah?"

"The next day she acted like nothing happened—ignored the fact that it happened. It was awkward."

"Have you brought up the kiss again?"

Harvey shook his head.

"You need to bring it up."

Harvey's gaze met his. "Yeah?"

"Yeah, either she'll appreciate your boldness and jump your bones, or you can laugh it off and move on."

Harvey nodded. "I'll think about it. Thanks for the advice. Hey, I'll see you in thirty?"

"I hope so, Harvey."

Nick stepped out onto the street and zipped up his jacket. It was a cold November night. He smiled as he remembered this time last year when he took Lauren out for their fake public date. Amazing what could change in one year. He thought for sure he'd be out of Fisher Springs by now, but here he was, right where he belonged.

He walked down the main street and rounded the corner. Harrow Accounting came into view. Lauren had decorated the window for the holidays. That was something he loved about this small town. She met him at the door.

"Perfect timing," she said.

He pulled her in for a deep kiss. "Ready?"

"Always."

He drove them to the seasonal ice rink and parked.

"What are we doing here?" she asked.

"Remember last year when we came here to put on a show for everyone? I thought this year we could be low key and enjoy the ice. Maybe this can be our annual tradition."

Her eyes lit up. "I like that."

Ten minutes later, they were out on the ice. He held her steady, just like before.

"Well, it's not exactly like last year," Lauren said.

"No?" He spun around in front of her and slowly pulled her toward the middle.

"No. Thanksgiving dinner with your family was much more pleasant."

He laughed. "I'm happy for that. My family understands that Sam isn't the one for me. You are."

They were in the middle of the rink. Suddenly, the music paused, all of the skaters stopped skating, and a spotlight shone down on them.

Lauren looked around. "What's going on?"

"I brought you back here because this is where it really all began. Yes, we argued at the mansion, but the night I brought you here was the night I knew I was falling for you."

"Nick, what are you doing?"

"Let me get this out."

"But, Nick—"

"Lauren, this is not the time to argue. Let me propose, dammit."

She gasped and her hands went to her mouth.

"Shit. I didn't mean to blurt that out. All right, what I meant to say was, that night I knew I was falling for you. And a year later, I've completely fallen for you. I can't imagine a life without you here in Fisher Springs. Lauren, will you marry me?"

All of the skaters were now holding sparklers and skating in a circle around them. Lauren's eyes welled with tears as she took it all in.

"Wait, is that safe? Fire on the ice?"

"Lauren?" Nick said through gritted teeth. "I asked you a question."

"Seriously, I think that's a safety issue."

"Woman…"

The widest grin spread across her face and he chuckled. Even in a moment like this, she had to pull his chain.

"Yes, Nick. Yes, I will marry you."

He picked her up and twirled her around as everyone surrounding them clapped and cheered. "God, I love you. You infuriate yet turn me on like no other, and I can't wait to spend the rest of my life with you."

"I love you too, Nick Moore, and I promise to spend the rest of my life deflating that big head of yours."

He threw his head back, laughing. "Luke told me he said that. I owe him one."

"Hey! Are you two done? It's cold out here. Let's get to the after-party!" Harmony yelled from across the ice.

Harvey was standing behind her, rubbing her arms.

"Is it me or do they look very cozy?" Lauren asked.

Nick gave Harvey a nod. "Yes, they do."

Chasing Her Trust

Other books by Danielle Pays

The Dare to Risk series

Deceived

Pursued

Played

Consumed

The Dare to Surrender series

Chasing Her Trust

Taking Her Chase

Saving Her Target

Trusting Her Hero

Captivated – A Dare to Risk/Dare to Surrender Crossover Holiday Novella

Chasing Her Trust

Chasing Her Trust

About the Author

Danielle Pays writes steamy romantic suspense with twists you won't see coming. She enjoys romance as well as mystery and suspense and blends them both using her beloved Pacific Northwest for inspiration with its mix of small towns and cities.

When she's not writing her characters into some kind of trouble, she can be found binging Netflix shows, trying to convince her children to eat her cooking, or drinking wine after battling said children at dinnertime.

Follow her at www.daniellepays.com or on Facebook at https://www.facebook.com/daniellepays/

CPSIA information can be obtained
at www.ICGtesting.com
Printed in the USA
LVHW030949170721
692931LV00002B/118